In Treason's Track

by

Albert Payson Terhune

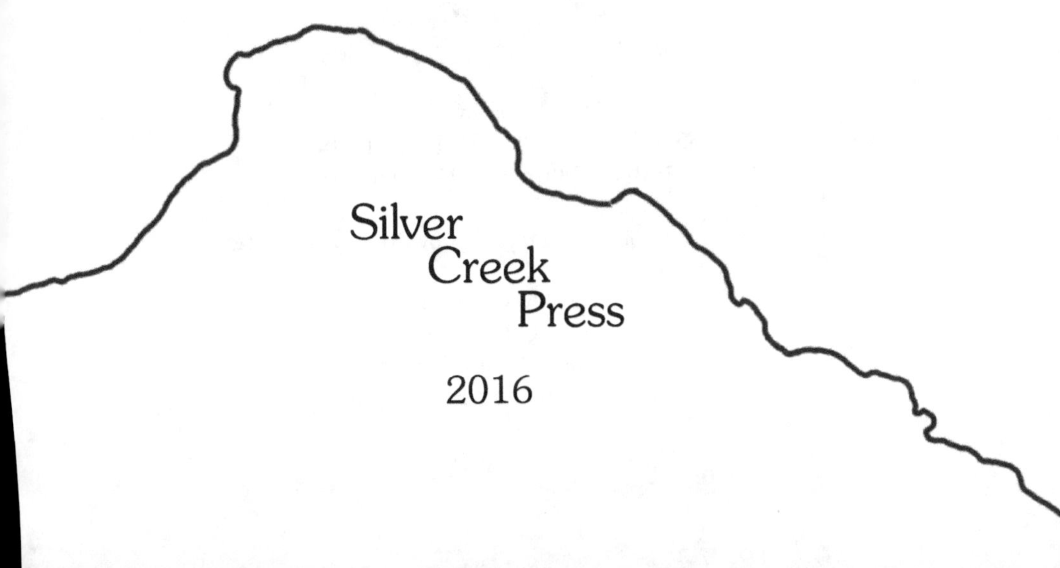

Silver
Creek
Press

2016

In Treason's Track
ISBN: 978-0-9967194-8-3 (paperback)
ISBN: 978-0-9967194-9-0 (ebook)

Book compilation and design by Rodney Schroeter

The Silver Creek Press
PO Box 334
Random Lake WI 53075-0334
rschroeter@silentreels.com

In Treason's Track

Chapter I.
The Girl in the Boat.

I WAS the most miserable man in the thirteen colonies!

I wanted to get away, to be by myself, to ponder over the cruel way fate was using me. If I stayed around headquarters another minute I knew I should be picking a quarrel with some talkative fellow officer.

Then, hey! for drawn swords, an exchange of thrusts, and—a fortnight in guard-house by way of penalty.

So it was that I stalked away from General Benedict Arnold's headquarters at the Beverly Robinson house below Cold Spring, and made my aimless way southwestward toward the river.

As I walked I drew out again the tinted, perfumed little letter the morning courier had brought me. I read it once more, though I already knew it by heart, and as I read my anger boiled afresh.

I nursed my thousand grievances as a peevish child might perversely bite hard upon a sore tooth.

The Hudson, at last, flashed blue and gold at my very feet. Scarce a hundred yards beyond stood the Robinson boathouse. A long row might well bring me to my senses, or at least show me a solution to my wretched perplexities.

Toward the boat-house I turned my steps. But, as I reached it, I halted with a scowl. There was seemingly no end to my ill luck this day. Where six skiffs, large and small, usually lay, there was now not one. Every boat had been preempted by earlier oarsmen.

As I stood there, I noted the last skiff of the lot, just making its way out of the tiny dock. In the nearest rower's bench sat a girl—slender, tall, graceful—handling the heavy oars with more than usual skill.

She was plainly clad in gray homespun, but the sunbeams nestled lovingly in the uncovered masses of her soft yellow hair. She was backing the boat out from the slip when first I saw her. But as the craft cleared the dock, she turned. Then I recognized her. She was Mistress Edith Bliss, the new governess that Madam Arnold had employed to teach her young stepson.

I had met the girl but once, for a moment, a few days earlier. Madam Arnold (with a mischievous twinkle in her merry eyes at forcing me to speak to a mere dependent) had introduced me to her. I had but mumbled a word of stiff acknowledgment and passed on.

Now, the sight of this provincial governess abstracting the only remaining boat and thus robbing me of my coveted row, was well-nigh too much for my self-control.

I was, for the instant, minded to growl out an order to her to come back and turn over the boat to me, chiding her for daring to take what her betters might need.

But ill-tempered as I was, I could scarce bring myself to do so churlish a thing. Moreover, though I knew Edith Bliss to be merely the over-educated daughter of a Cold Spring farmer, there was something so daintily aristocratic about her bearing, as she manipulated the heavy oars, that I somehow could not speak the words of reproof that I should have used to an ordinary servant.

Just then her eyes met mine. Her face flushed with genuine pleasure, and she waved a hand to me in gay salute. It was as though a lonely child had all at once seen a welcome playmate.

I glowered sulkily back at her. But my scowl had no lessening effect upon her bright smile of greeting. Indeed, she quite misinterpreted my look.

"Good morning, Captain Wayne," she called pleasantly. "I don't wonder you look so glum. You came down here to go rowing, didn't you? And here I am running away with the very last boat."

"It's of no consequence," I grumbled, with all the suave courtesy of a sick bear.

"Oh, but it *is*," she retorted laughingly. "You want to go rowing. So do I. There is only one boat. Hence, there is only one way out of the difficulty. We will go together!"

I stared down at her with a cold haughtiness that went wholly unobserved. She was again turning the boat and backing shoreward.

"Wait till I bring it alongside the slip," she cried, panting with the exertion. "One more stroke will do it. *So!*"

The boat was cleverly maneuvered so that its gunwale was at my very feet. Mistress Bliss's face smiled a bright invitation to me. I was busy coining some phrase of crushing reproof when—all of a sudden I found myself actually stepping down into the skiff.

No, I have not the remotest idea how it happened. Whether the girl's glance mesmerized me, or whether the odd childlikeness of her nature made me hesitate at hurting her feelings.

The moment I was in the boat I was mightily minded to scramble out again. But, such a course would have fitted ill with my sullen dignity. I seated myself at the central thwart and quickly caught up the oars.

Mistress Bliss, with the happy little laugh of a child who is being taken out for a holiday, settled herself in the stern and leaned back with ineffable content.

I hoped none of my snobbish fellow officers would see me thus playing carpet knight to a governess in homespun. The thought irritated me. I bent to the long oars with a series of strokes that sent the boat fairly dancing along the river's placid surface.

The month was September, in the year of grace 1780. Across the sunlit stream loomed West Point, crowned with its grim line of fortifications. To north and south on either side frowned the rampart-lined Highlands of the Hudson.

In the distance somewhere a regimental band was playing. The sound reached us clearly through the warm air.

"How beautiful everything is!" sighed the girl in dreamy rapture, "and how wonderful. Oh, it is good to be alive!"

I made no answer, but dug my oar-blades harder into the water.

"How well you row," she commented. "I never was rowed so fast before. You must have the strength of a giant."

Breathes there a man so deaf to flattery that a compliment to his strength does not touch him in a tender spot? If so, I am not that man.

I still spoke no word, but I slightly relaxed my sulky scowl of haughty aloofness.

The girl was really pretty. And she had a grace of manner that any woman might well have envied. It was a pity that she was a governess, a farmer's daughter.

"Isn't this delightful?" she murmured. "Just to lean back and be rowed so fast on the loveliest river in the world, and on a day like this! It isn't every girl who could get the famous Captain Philip Wayne to take her rowing."

I glanced suspiciously at her from under my frowning brows. Was she making fun of me? Would she dare?

No, her flower face showed only child-like pleasure.

"Why do you frown when I call you 'famous' Captain Wayne?" she queried. "You are famous, you know. Madam Arnold told me all about you. She told how you won a lieutenancy at Ticonderoga, how you saved General Arnold's life, by cutting down the *voyageur* who was attacking him when he was wounded at Quebec; how you charged at his side in the glorious battle of Saratoga, and won there a captaincy through sheer bravery. Yes," she added, "and the havoc you played with the pretty Tory girls' hearts when General Arnold was in command at Philadelphia that winter, too. There was one girl, Madam Arnold says, who—"

"If you please," I broke in harshly, "I would rather not discuss my private affairs with a stranger. I—"

"A stranger?" she echoed. "But *we* aren't strangers. Madam Arnold introduced us very formally, only last week. Oh, look! There, away to the south. There's a sloop of war. I didn't know—"

"It's the Vulture. A British war sloop. It has run up from New York two or three times. No one knows why."

I checked myself. I had not meant to unbend so far as to converse with this very forward governess. I was angry at my own breach of silence, and I cast about me for a few well-chosen words that should teach her her place.

"Look out!" she warned. "Hard-aport! *So.* You nearly ran into the red buoy. It lies so low and the glare on the water is so strong that I didn't see it till we were almost right on it."

I scowled at the low-floating globe of scarlet, with its crisscross of chains. Then I rowed on.

"You are rowing so fast," she commented, "that if we had struck the buoy, our prow might have been stove in.

"Then, just think of what might have happened! A full mile from shore and not a boat in sight to rescue us. Could you swim a mile, Captain Wayne?"

"No," I snapped.

It had always been a sore point with me that, strong as I am in other respects, I can never swim more than half a mile at most without cramps.

"How lucky, then," she laughed gaily, "that we didn't have an accident! *I* can swim a mile—I *think* I can—but I'm quite sure I couldn't carry *you* all that distance. Wouldn't we look funny—you a great giant of an officer, being towed into port by a girl like me? You would have to marry me out of gratitude. People always do, in books, you know."

Her utterly innocent speech, born of high good humor and a youthful spirit of fun, ripped out my last barriers of breeding. Still pulling away at the oars with all my might, I burst forth angrily:

"Mistress Bliss! When you chose, this morning, to forget our widely different positions and to presume on my good nature to make me take you rowing, I overlooked it. But surely a woman of discernment should have seen by now that I do not care to converse with you. I have tried to spare your feelings by indicating this instead of putting it into plain words. But when your speech becomes impertinently familiar as it did just now, I must—"

"Oh!"

There was a world of meaning in the soft-gasped little monosyllable that cut short my brutal tirade. There was infinitely more in the flushed face that met mine in such pained wonder.

Dumb amazement, a poignant incredulity, grief—all battled for expression in her one word and in her big pansy-colored eyes.

All at once, I felt as if some laughing five-year-old child had come running toward me with a gift and as if I had struck the advancing youngster with my clenched fist.

This girl was so innocent, so immature! She had hailed with joy the prospect of a row on the river with a man whose few paltry war deeds she had magnified into heroism. She had done her best to entertain me, ignoring my black looks, until, (with no provocation that she could understand) I had rebuked her as I would scarce have rebuked a swearing, drunken trooper.

Oh, I assure you, I felt like a cur. Had she flamed into wrath or even burst into loud weeping, I should hardly have felt less badly.

But she only looked at me in anguished, amazed disbelief. I racked my brain for something to say that might soften the blow. But I sat there tongue-tied.

It was she who spoke first. Very quietly, in a subdued crushed little voice, she said:

"I am sorry. I didn't understand. Will you please take me back now? I wish to go home."

I tried to mumble some sort of an apology, but again my tongue refused its office. Putting the boat about, I headed back for the eastern shore, throwing even greater force into my strokes, as I sought for words to excuse my crass brutality.

Now, as is usually the case when it is too late—I saw the utter harmlessness of all the girl had said and done. And I saw how my own ill-temper and misfortunes had led me to vent upon her the rage that fate's repeated bad treatment had aroused in me.

She was so young, so pretty, so childish! And she had been having such a beautiful time there on the river, during the brief interval of leisure from teaching young Arnold. I had spoiled it all.

"Mistress Bliss," I began, "I—"

Then I stopped. She was sitting with averted head. I could have kicked myself. I gave one desperate tug at the oars that embodied all my self-contempt. And then—

A quick jar. The boat stopped with a thud. The prow jumped high out of water. The port gunwale careened sharply. A cry from the girl. And I pitched overboard.

I had a momentary glimpse of a network of rusted chains just beneath the surface. Then my head smote the nearest one with a whack that sent my five wits a scattering.

Chapter II.
Marooned.

I FELT my body lurch into the cool water and sink.

Dully I knew, I had rowed at full speed into the red buoy that I had so narrowly missed on the outward trip. But this time Edith Bliss's eyes had been too tear-filled to note the danger.

The impact of my head against the chain had not wholly stunned me. But it seemed to have jarred some nerve center. Momentarily helpless to move, I was none the less well aware that I had fallen over-board, that the heat of the upper air had been replaced by a delicious wet coolness, that I was quietly sinking down—*down.*

In due time, I incoherently knew, I should begin to rise again. When I should reach the surface I might be able to shake off my numbness and strike out.

In the meanwhile I was drowsy and cared little what might happen. I wonder now that I had the sense to hold my breath.

Down I went, a million miles or more—seemingly. Then my body paused (the force of my plunge being at length counteracted by the upbearing power of the water) and started slowly upward.

It had risen but a foot or two when it came to a grating stop, neatly caught under one of the projecting chains that ran down to the shoal at the river bottom.

There I hung, helpless. My only strong sensations were a yearning to breathe and an instinct that I must not. My senses were coming back. But my power to move was still in abeyance.

And there, caught under water like any soaked bit of driftwood, I bade fair to remain until I should drown.

I probably had not been immersed more than thirty seconds. And a man can hold breath much longer than that. But, to my returning consciousness, it seemed an eternity. And my lungs ached to bursting.

No, I did not review in lightning panorama every event of my past life. I was too much stupefied. I merely realized the full peril of my plight and tried in vain to rid my memory of the haunting vision of two big gentle tear-filled eyes.

Then through the green coolness of the water something flashed. It seemed a quivering maze of brown and white and gold.

I had a fleeting, brief glimpse of a little face from which a pair of pansy-colored eyes gazed weirdly at me.

A wrench from some unseen hand and my body, freed from its helpless position beneath the chain, shot upward.

To the surface I popped, sputtering and drawing in great breaths of the warm sunlit air. My strength, too, was beginning to come back, and I began to struggle with feeble inefficiency.

But, even as my eyes cleared of the water and I glanced about me, a golden head shot above the surface, not far from my side.

And in the dripping, glowing mermaid who swam up to me I recognized Edith Bliss.

Already my weak efforts to move were pulling me once more below the surface. With one strong white little hand, Mistress Bliss caught hold of my collar and held my head above water.

"Can you move?" she asked.

"A very little," I gasped, "I'm—"

"Turn over on your back and lie rigid!" she ordered.

With difficulty, and chiefly by her help, I obeyed. With a twist of her lithe body, she got one shoulder under mine. Bearing me up thus, she struck out strongly.

"You—you can't swim all the way to shore with me," I murmured.

"I am making for the boat," she answered between strokes.

A moment later her arm flashed out of the water and caught the side of the skiff. We had risen a bare ten feet from the gunwale, but my back had been toward it. Clinging to my shoulder with one hand and to the boat with the other, she rested for a moment.

"I don't understand," said she. "The skiff ought to careen under this weight, but it is as firm as a rock. Oh, I see now! The bow is so firmly jammed between two buoy-chains that it can't stir. You were rowing fast, and the impetus wedged the boat tightly among the chains. Do you think you are strong enough now to hold on to the side?"

"I'm all right again," I announced, seizing the gunwale.

And I was. As is often the case with temporary paralysis to nerve centers, my strength was returning as suddenly as it had left me. I was still a trifle shaky, but in moderately full possession of my big muscles.

"I'll get aboard and help you in," I volunteered, beginning to wriggle across the gunwale.

But she did not wait for me. She was over the side and in the boat before I had half accomplished the same task. Then she turned to help me.

Ordinarily it is no easy feat to board a rowboat in midstream, but so securely was our skiff caught in the angle of two big chains that it did not so much as move as we scrambled aboard. The prow was high out of water and the stern almost awash. The deep keel near the bow was the part wedged in the chains.

I dropped into the tilting bottom of the skiff and looked up at

Edith Bliss, who had perched on one of the slanted thwarts.

Her hair had come loose from its fastenings and flowed in a mass of shimmering gold nearly to her knees. Her face glowed with her violent exertions. Her wet clothes hung about her like antique drapery. Never had I beheld so wondrously beautiful a sight.

"You were thrown out," she was saying. "So was I, but I caught the gunwale and saved myself from going under. You didn't come up. I remembered the chains, and I guessed what had happened. So I dived for you."

"You—you saved my life," I muttered.

"Oh," she said lightly, "even impertinent strangers have their uses."

"Forgive me," I cried, all penitence. "What could have made me speak so to you? I could almost wish I had stayed under water, now that I remember what I said—and what you have done in return. Believe me, I am not a boor always."

At my first words of bungling contrition her face brightened as does a child's when a peevish schoolmate "makes up" a quarrel.

"You don't have to apologize any more," she said gently, "but I'm glad you're sorry. And I'm glad—very, *very* glad—I was able to help you out of the water. Now, we're good friends again, aren't we?"

Her utter simplicity no longer jarred upon me. Instead, I found something vaguely delicious in it.

Our eyes met. To both of us came all at once the realization of our sopping, bedraggled condition, of our isolation there in a tip-tilted boat in mid-river.

I do not know why it was, but suddenly we both broke into loud, uncontrollable laughter. The sound of our mirth rolled out over the silent, bright waters. We laughed until the tears rolled down our cheeks, until we were panting and weak.

Partly, perhaps, it was reaction; partly the sight of each other's weird aspect, partly—I know not what. But this I know: that wave of wholesome laughter cleared the mental air like a thunder-storm and left us far closer together, in acquaintance, than a whole year of ordinary intercourse could have done.

At last I rose, cautiously wiping the tears of merriment from my eyes, and looked about me. On every side the shining river stretched out under the hot September sun. No sign of craft anywhere.

"We are marooned," I announced.

"I don't understand," she answered.

"We are stuck here," I explained, vainly probing at the chains with an oar, trying to shake the boat free. "We can't get off. We can't swim as far as the nearest shore. We are south of the military posts, and, even if we weren't, I doubt if a hail from us could be heard by any one on shore. I can't see another boat. Here we are, and here we stay—indefinitely."

"But surely," she laughed, "we will be seen from land."

"Our boat will be seen perhaps, but what good will that do? At such a distance it will seem as if we are anchored here, fishing."

"But some other boat will come along—"

"In course of time, doubtless; but the Hudson, just below West Point, is not the Hudson just below Wall Street in New York. There may be a boat that will pass in hailing distance during the next ten minutes. On the other hand, there may not be one that will come near enough to notice us within three days. That's what I meant when I said we are marooned. Luckily the weather is so hot we aren't likely to take a chill from our wetting."

I set to work stripping off my uniform coat. I rigged it to the blade of a long oar and managed to fasten the oar-handle upright between two cleats.

The impromptu signal-flag hung limp and dripping under the hot sun.

"Our vigil has begun," I remarked.

"We are shipwrecked mariners on a desert island," she answered gleefully. "Isn't it fun?"

"After the first day or two the humor of it may begin to pall," I ventured to suggest.

Chapter III.
A Story of Ill Luck.

THERE we sat, as helpless and as merry as a pair of truant babies, chatting away as though we had known each other all our lives.

Meantime our clothes slowly dried upon us, and at intervals I rose to scan the river for sign of approaching boats. In circumstances like those one cannot be formal, try as ever so hard. And I did not try. We talked of a dozen indifferent topics, and laughed at things that were not of deep wit.

For the moment I had forgotten my myriad woes, my grievance against fate, my hopeless future. I was content to be *young* with this childlike girl. It was she, at last, who brought me back to the memory of my own worries.

"Captain Wayne," she said a little timidly, "I don't want to be impertinent, but I wish I could help you."

"Help me? How?"

"When I saw you at the boat-house this morning," she went on, still a little shyly, "your face was so sad, so troubled! It made my heart ache for you. That is why I asked you to come rowing. I thought maybe it would cheer you up. And while you rowed you looked so miserable; I tried to get your mind off your bothers by talking nonsense. Then you reproved me. And—"

"That is cruel," I interrupted; "you forgave my boorishness. Won't you try to forget it?"

"It *wasn't* boorishness," she contradicted prettily. "It wasn't even bad temper. I see that now it just meant you were unhappy. And you were too miserable to bear being disturbed. So when I spoke—"

"You are sweet and charitable," said I, "but I was a boor, just the same."

"Have it as you will," she conceded with a smile. "If it comforts you to misjudge yourself, pray continue to. But—you were unhappy. Cannot you tell me about it? I might help."

For a moment the old resentment at her familiarity swept across me, but we had passed the stage where non-acquaintance rears formal barriers.

Besides, no man at heart can deny that there is a temptation to pour one's woes into a pretty woman's ears. And Edith Bliss was looking at me with a tender—almost motherly—appeal that I could not withstand.

Thus it was that I found myself talking in a horribly confidential way to a lovely girl whom I scarcely knew, telling her things I had never thought to reveal to any one.

I make no excuse for this. Let him who has never confided impulsively in a woman judge me. I think I shall then go unjudged.

"It is no *one* annoyance," I said lamely, "but the accumulation of a dozen. Here is the tale in brief:

"When the Revolution began, five years ago, I was a rising young lawyer in New York. I was of good Tory family. I had bright prospects. I was barely twenty-five. I threw over everything to take up arms for my country."

"Good!" she cried. "My father did the same thing. He—"

"If he regrets it as much as I do," I said, "he has my pity."

"He *never* regretted, it," she answered softly. "He—he died at Valley Forge—not fighting a mortal enemy, but starving and freezing for liberty's sake. Yet he felt no regret."

Her simple words of faith touched me. Yet, with memory of my own misfortunes, I hurried on:

"I cast in my fortunes with Benedict Arnold. He was my family's friend. He liked me. He promised that as he rose, so should I rise. And to the best of his ability he kept his word. But what can he do for me—for *any one?*"

"He is a friend of General Washington. The dear friend. He—"

"That is his chief misfortune," I said bitterly. "Conway, Gates, and the rest, who hate Washington, vent their spite by injuring Arnold, his friend, knowing in that way they can strike most cruelly at the chief's great heart. Washington's enemies in Congress, too, are forever seeking means of disgracing Arnold so that they may pain Washington. It has been so since the very beginning. Until I have wondered that General Arnold endures it. A less gallant patriot than he would long ago have broken his sword, or might even have gone over to the British."

"Shame!" she cried. "You do not mean that. No one but a traitor—"

"Perhaps you do not know the whole story as I know it," said I. "From the very start it was so. Arnold was sent to take Ticonderoga. I went with him as a sub-lieutenant. On the way Ethan Allen and his 'Green Mountain Boys' joined us. The whole expedition was Arnold's idea. Yet Allen was given command over his head, and to Allen went the chief glory of the victory. Arnold made the fearful wilderness journey to Quebec.

"Again, Congress's lack of cooperation robbed him of victory and of reward. Five junior officers were made major-generals, while he went for months unpromoted. At Saratoga, while Gates was wrangling with his staff in his own tent, it was Arnold who led the victorious charge that crushed Burgoyne's army. Yet to Gates did Congress give the whole glory, and Arnold is still unrewarded."

"But he was made commander at Philadelphia that year. Surely that—"

"That was the direct work of General Washington in opposition to Congress's wishes. Scarcely had Arnold assumed command in Philadelphia when his enemies set secretly to work. They trumped up vile charges of dishonesty against him and forced him to trial. *Him*—the hero of Saratoga! Every serious charge was disproven. Yet Congress was not content, but ordered General Washington to insult Arnold by a public reprimand."

"I remember," she answered; "but the chief made that reprimand so gentle that it was almost a compliment."

"Yet, the shame of it remained. To make up to his friend for such bitter injustice, Washington has put Arnold here in charge of West Point—the strongest fortress we have, the key to our whole strength, the place on whose safety our fate hangs. But even now the foes in Congress and the army are at work to harm him. And Arnold has borne it all. He is the true hero of this Revolution of ours. No other man, save Washington alone, deserves so highly of his country, and none has been so ill-used. I marvel that he does not seek revenge. It is scarce in human nature not to."

"Captain Wayne," said she suddenly, "you have been most eloquent in your commander's behalf. Yet we have strayed far afield in our talk. Methinks it was your grievances, not General Arnold's, that we began to speak of."

"Mine are his," I retorted. "In more senses than one. Not only do I resent the injustice done to my friend and leader, but, as his fortunes are my fortunes, I have shared in his ill luck. I have been in the army five years. I threw away a good profession for my country's sake. Other men who have done less service, and who have risked far less, have risen high in rank. Because I am an Arnold man I am still a mere captain, with no hope of further promotion. Five years thrown away!"

"No, no," she protested hotly. "Five years of glorious service in liberty's cause. Yet," she added more softly, "I scarce wonder you grow bitter at times. Still, in the end, when our country at last is free—"

"Free?" I scoffed. "It will never be free. The Revolution is doomed. Arnold himself secretly admits that. For five years we have fought on with varying success. And victory is farther away from us now than it was in 1776 when we signed our useless Declaration of Independence. We shall struggle along hopelessly a little longer. Then we will be forced to yield to—"

"*Yield?*" she cried, her face aflame. "Never, *never!* Not while George Washington leads us."

"Fine words," I muttered. "But the end is in sight. Even Arnold sees that. We cannot hold out much longer. We have no money. We have few men. Before long, by sheer force of numbers, England will force us to our knees. For my own part, I am half inclined to do as my parents begged me to, and go over to the enemy. In a year or so, at most, that is what all of us will have to do."

"*Horrible!*" she panted. "How dare you speak so?"

Already I was ashamed of my pettish outburst. Angry and discontented as I was, yet in my heart of hearts I knew I would shed the last drop of my blood for my stricken country sooner than turn a traitor.

Yet, after the way of angry men, it just then pleased me to talk like a fool. And the girl's indignation served but to make me the more stubborn.

"It is easy for you to chide me," I sneered. "You are a woman. You have not fought and hoped and planned and toiled for five years as I have—and all for nothing."

"No," she returned, "yet my father died for liberty. And my two brothers fell, one at Bunker Hill and one at Saratoga. The Revolution has left me penniless and—alone. Perhaps, in a way, this glorious struggle for liberty has cost us women as much as it has cost you men. But I know you cannot mean what you say about betraying your country by going over to the enemy. I should as soon think of suspecting General Arnold himself."

We fell silent for a space, while again I scanned the waters for passing craft. It was she who first spoke.

"I thank you, Captain Wayne," she said, "for telling me all this. I wish I might help you to bear it as so gallant a man should. But—if I am not mistaken—there was more than a mere chronic grievance against fate that so darkened your brow to-day. Was there not? I may be wrong, but I have a foolish womanly intuition that you have not even touched upon your chief trouble."

I looked at her half in resentment. And again something in those big, childlike eyes impelled me.

"I spent the winter at Philadelphia," I said awkwardly, "on General Arnold's staff. It was my first glimpse of civilized life since this wretched war set in. We had a gay, care-free time. The general kept open house, especially after he married Mistress Shippen. There was much social gaiety. Also, there was a girl—"

"I *knew* it!" proclaimed Edith Bliss.

Yet in her announcement there was less triumph at her own prophetic powers than might have been expected.

"A Mistress Dorothy Cary," I resumed. "Of the Chestnut Street Carys, a great Tory family of Philadelphia. Half the officers of the staff were daft with love for her. So was I. She—she favored me. Or so I dared hope. There was no betrothal. Yet—I dreamed of success. Last month I took heart and wrote, beseeching her to be my wife."

"Yes?" queried Edith as I paused; and once more I noted a strange lack of life in her sweet voice.

"I weary you with my stupid love-tale?" I asked.

"No," she denied. "No. Go on."

"And," I answered, fishing from my waistcoat pocket a damp, crumpled scrap of tinted, perfumed paper, "this morning the answer came."

Edith was leaning forward, her lips slightly parted.

"How women dote on hearing of a romance!" commented I fatuously.

Then, more seriously, I added:

"The gist of the letter is this: She esteems me highly. She likes me better, she says, than any other man she knows. She might even readily learn to love me. But—"

"Ah!"

"But she would die before she would wed an enemy of her country."

"She is English? "

"No," I said; "a Tory. She regards England as her country, and deems all Revolutionists base rebels who merit hanging. Her verdict is this," I continued, glancing again at the wet note, "if I will renounce the patriot cause and join the English army she will be my wife. Otherwise she desires never to see me or hear from me again."

"Oh, *poor* Captain Wayne!" cried Edith in quick, warm sympathy. "The cruel, unjust woman!"

"No," I contradicted, "she is but loyal. And—the choice she offers me is very tempting. I scarce know what to do."

"You well know what to do!" she retorted. "You will do your duty as a valiant, true man. Your heart may break, but you will stand by the cause."

She looked very lovely—like some Norse goddess of old—as she thus bade me obey conscience and turn my back on love. A wild, insane, wholly inexplicable impulse seized me as I gazed on her.

Something of my feelings must have shone from my eyes. For a red flame leaped to her cheeks.

"Edith—Mistress Bliss," I began, "I—"

"Skiff ahoy!" roared a voice not fifty feet away. "What's amiss?"

A fisherman's shallop was bearing down upon us.

Chapter IV.
On the Neutral Ground.

OF course, it was my lot that the rescuing fisherman's boat should set us two ashore at the Robinson boat-house at the precise moment when no less than five officers of the post and a couple of my fellow-staff members happened to be passing.

They doffed their hats in ironically low salutes as we walked through their parted group. And they eyed with merry wonder our bedraggled condition.

Their gaze and their thin-veiled amusement served to bring me back to my senses with a shock.

For an hour or more I had been babbling like a garrulous school-boy, telling this almost stranger-girl the most secret and sacred things of my life. I, who was ever reserved as regards my own affairs, had let an unusual situation and a pair of pansy eyes turn my private history inside out.

Nay, worse. I had done a monstrous imprudent thing. I had openly babbled mutiny to her. I had prophesied the Revolution's failure. I had said I was sick of my profession as a Continental officer. I had spoken as though I actually intended to desert to the enemy.

Now, were she by any chance a spy (and there were perforce many such on both sides in those days) she might well ruin me by repeating one-half of what I, in my peevishness, had blurted out.

The idea was not pleasant. One so often says things to a woman that he would find hard to account for were they repeated later to men.

I waxed troubled. I glanced covertly at the tall, gaily-chatting girl at my side, as we both wended our way toward headquarters.

The moment's glamour—the midsummer madness—were quite gone. Once more I was the somewhat arrogant, birth-proud Philip Wayne, spoiled by a winter of Philadelphia gaiety and by subsequent alternate petting and neglect.

The girl beside me was no longer the bewitching mermaid—the Norse goddess companion of my marooning—but once more a farmer's daughter, a dependent of my commander's wife.

And it was to this mere employee, this daughter of the soil, that I had unburdened my heart! I felt sick and ashamed. For a man's nature does not wholly and permanently change in a single hour.

Edith seemed to notice my alteration of manner. It puzzled her at first. Then, with sudden concern, she cried:

"You have caught cold? The wetting was too much for you? And here I am making you walk slowly to keep pace with me, when you ought to be hurrying on to your quarters to get a change of clothing. How careless of me!"

With a bright smile and a nod of friendly farewell, she slipped through a gap in the hedge, struck a footpath that led direct to the Robinson house, and ran on, leaving me to follow the main road to the officers' quarters.

I stared after her a moment. Her grace and her utter friendliness again threatened momentarily to upset my stiff ideas of our relative positions in life. But, even as I, half shamefacedly, made as though to follow her, a voice at my elbow checked me.

"So might the dripping river god stare after the flying wood-nymph!" intoned some one with mock solemnity. "Now, out and alas! that the high-born and most severely punctilious Captain Philip Wayne should stoop to cast sheep's eyes after a pretty governess!"

I turned. A slender, gaily-dressed young man stood laughing pleasantly at my frowning surprise. I had not expected to see him here. He was Alexander Hamilton, General Washington's own secretary.

Washington had gone two days earlier to confer with the Count de Rochambeau at Hartford, and Hamilton had gone with him. So had the young French Marquis de la Fayette. None of the party were expected back for another fortnight.

"You are on leave?" I asked, ignoring Hamilton's mischievous grin.

"On leave?" he echoed. "We of his excellency's personal staff get scant 'leave,' I can tell you. No, I was sent back with papers of his for General Arnold. I arrived half an hour agone; only to find Arnold is making a tour of the Catskill forts and will not be back for a day or so. I was just starting to rejoin his excellency when I beheld a fish-boat drawing toward shore laden with a cargo of two youthful and beauteous creatures; very wet, but seemingly very happy."

"Have done!" I begged. "I—"

"I thought to see shepherd and shepherdess," he went on, unheeding. "Then I recognized your worthy and dignified self. 'Forsooth,' thought I, 'the maid he has deigned to honor with his companionship must sure be a countess at very least!' But alack! I was wrong. 'Twas a simple governess in homespun clad. Lad, I rejoice to see you so human. You have shown excellent taste. She is most fair. And, Madam Arnold tells me, she has a brain as well. When are the nuptials to be?"

With a growl I turned on my heel and stalked away. I sought to look dignified and stately, but a dripping uniform, wet hair, and boots filled with water are but poor aids to stately dignity.

I was far from being at the end of my persecutions. All that day and the next I was the butt of every hare-brained officer in the whole messroom. More cheap wit was lavished at my expense than I had thought the entire Continental army possessed.

Because I refused to give any reason for my appearance with

Edith, in the fisherman's boat, every man had a theory of his own to account for it.

One portly major gravely suggested that Edith had fallen into the water off the boathouse; that I had plunged in to her rescue; that I had then been so much in love I had forgotten on which side of the river I belonged and had forthwith swum with her across the Hudson to West Point and was on my way back when we were picked up.

A pert subaltern vowed that I had leaped into the river with her in my arms and that I had refused to bring her ashore until she should promise to wed me.

"And," added the subaltern, "since she had too much sense to accept, there they would have stayed until the Hudson froze over, had not sanity, in the form of an honest fisherman, saved them from an eternal bath."

These were but two of a dozen lame jests I was forced to endure. I have spoken of them so that it may be understood to what pitch of mind I came. Like every other man on earth, I can never abide a joke at my own expense.

And, being a young fool, all these gibes made me but the angrier with the innocent cause of it all—Edith Bliss. That was why, as you shall see, when the time came, I once more behaved like a cur.

And—as you will still later see, I was to be well punished.

It was two days later that Madam Arnold invited a half dozen of us officers and as many ladies from the neighborhood, to a picnic at Garrison's Spring, a picturesque, romantic woodland spot some few miles south of headquarters, and on the edge of the wide strip of territory known in those war-times as the "Neutral Ground."

The British held New York City and the land for some miles to the northward of it. The Americans held the West Point region and on both sides of the river. Almost the whole eastern tract of the Hudson country from our lines to those of the British was a sort of No-Man's Land.

It was debatable territory, the scene of many a raid and skirmish. And it had taken the odd title of "Neutral Ground."

The picnic formed a jolly little break in our daily routine. We were a gay crowd, and Madam Arnold was the liveliest of hostesses. Edith Bliss was there. It was the first time I had seen her since our ducking in the river.

She bowed in laughing, inviting fashion across the heads of a dozen other guests, and beckoned me to join her. As she did so, I caught the amused glances of one or two officers.

I stiffened, bowed frigidly in reply to her friendly salute, and paid no attention whatever to her invitation.

Yes, I was a boor. A poor cad who feared ridicule from devoting himself to the loveliest woman in all that party.

I know that now. Dimly, I knew it then.

I was but a poor sort of hero. I misdoubt me you have discovered that for yourself ere now. But I have here set down my faults in crass frankness that you might the better understand the need of the fiery iron trials that later were to crush and efface the worst of those same faults.

Luncheon over, I strayed through the grove alone, for a quiet smoke, and to ponder afresh the cruel ultimatum Mistress Dorothy Cary's letter had offered me.

Somehow, to my bewilderment, I began of late to find myself less heartbroken over that fair maiden's coldness than I had once thought. I wondered at this.

I was perhaps a furlong away from the others when I threw myself down on a mossy mound, beside a woodland bridle-path, and relight-ed my pipe.

I could still hear the voices and laughter of the picnickers, although a screen of foliage wholly shut me off from their view.

I was drowsy, perhaps I dozed for a moment. I felt, all at once, that some one was looking down at me. I opened my eyes with a start. There, in the bridle-path before me, stood Edith Bliss.

I know not why it is that a man is always ashamed to have been caught sleeping. But so it is.

"Oh!" exclaimed Edith, "I woke you! I didn't mean to. You looked so big and so comfortable, all sprawled out there asleep. And you were actually *snoring!* As loudly as—"

"I beg your pardon," I growled, angrier than ever at this latest charge, "I regret that I should have made a spectacle of myself. I regret still more that you should have felt bound to seek me out to tell me so."

"There!" she complained in mimic fright, "you are cross again. As cross as can be. Please don't scowl," she went on appealingly. "I stole away from the rest for a chat with you. Isn't that a compliment?"

"I am sorry you took such trouble on my poor account," I muttered ungraciously.

"Trouble? Why, it was no trouble at all. I *wanted* to come. I would rather talk to you than to any other man at the post. Honestly, I would."

"I am afraid Madam Arnold will miss you," I began, straining my ears lest some wandering officer might come upon us and thus add a new chapter to the tale of mockery that had lately been my portion.

"Oh, she won't miss me," Edith reassured me. "I told her where I was going. She called me as I left the luncheon board. And I called back that I was going to look for you. They laughed. I wonder why?"

"Probably," I snarled, unreasonably stung by this new source of ridicule, "probably they laughed because it is not customary for any woman—even be she a provincial governess—to run in search of a man who has not sought her society and who does not—"

I stopped. She shrank back, with that same look of childlike dismay that once before had shamed me.

I was sorry. My lips were parted to tell her so, to say I did want her with me, that she was the loveliest and most innocently bewitching woman I had ever seen.

But, before the first eager, stammering word could be spoken, a man (who seemed to drop out of nowhere) quietly stepped between us.

Chapter V.
The Man of Mystery.

THE stranger had evidently advanced toward us along the bridle-path. He was leading a big roan horse. His steps and the footbeats of his mount had been muffled by the soft mold of the path.

He stepped between us, I say, without a word and in a manner of lofty authority that I vaguely resented.

He was of middle height, youthful, strikingly handsome, and with the unconscious, graceful air of a French aristocrat.

He wore civilian's riding-clothes, and a court sword dangled at his side. He would have seemed more in place (riding-clothes and all) in a ballroom than on this lonely by-track of Neutral Ground.

His face looked as if it was oftener gay than grave. But just now it was set and stern. He turned to Edith with a courtly bow.

"A thousand pardons for my intrusion," he said, "but as I drew near I heard this brute speak to you in a way that seemed to call for chastisement. Have I your gracious permission to punish him?"

His voice was pleasant, low-pitched, without the faintest trace of excitement. It was as though he had seen her trying in vain to manage a vicious dog and had offered to thrash the animal.

My face went scarlet with fury at his calm offer and his open contempt.

"No. No!" begged Edith, in panic, instinctively moving nearer to my side as though to protect me.

This finished the loss of my sanity. Whirling about on the stranger, I shouted hoarsely:

"Zounds! How dare you speak like this of an officer of the army? I'll flog you with your own riding-whip. If—"

"I had the honor of addressing this lady, sir," he answered, unruffled. "It pains me—as it must pain any man of breeding—to be forced to exchange speech with a yokel who can sink to speaking to a woman as you did, just now. I do not force you to apologize to her. For you are probably ignorant of the word's meaning. And as she intercedes to save you a thrashing, I have no redress but to let you go, though," he sighed gently, "it irks me to do it."

"How—I—"

"You spoke of yourself, I think," he went on, in that same soft, emotionless tone, "as an officer. The words 'officer' and 'gentleman' are ever supposed to go together. I grieve that, in your case, they can never hope to do so. No man with the remotest claim to decency could speak to a woman as you did. She seems inclined to submit to the insult. I cannot punish you against her orders, much as I long to. But be warned, I beg. Next time, some less considerate man than I may chance to overhear you. And then you may not escape the horsewhipping you so strongly need. Madam, your most obedient, sympathizing servant!"

Again he bowed, low with the grace of a true courtier, and made as though to mount his horse. But by this time my brain had cleared somewhat from the chaos caused by his mildly breathed words. Each gentle sentence had been worse than a kick to me.

The divergence between his speech and manner had momentarily dazed me into dumfounded silence. But now, boiling with rage at the man's treatment—and trebly so because Edith Bliss had been witness to it—I leaped forward with a cry to intercept him.

My saber was out. In one bound I was face to face with him, ablaze with hate, forgetful now of Edith's presence, mad to wipe out the memory of his insolent treatment.

"Draw!" I yelled. "Draw, or I'll split you like a fowl!"

He sighed. A genuine melancholy tinged his handsome face.

"I regret," said he sadly, "to soil my sword by contact with a boor's. I had hoped ever to keep it for gentlemen. Also, I am ashamed to brawl in the presence of a lady. I pray you let me pass on."

"You coward!" I raged. "You think to insult me and ride on alive? *Will* you draw, or will you take the flat of my blade across your face?"

"I see it is of no use," he said in sorrowful resignation, as he drew his sword. "Madam, in advance I crave your pardon. I shall not harm him."

Before the words were well out of his mouth I was upon him. A little cry of fear from Edith. Then our blades met with a clash.

I disengaged, and lunged ferociously for his throat. As he easily guarded the blow, his slender sword made a lightning-quick motion.

My heavy saber flew from my hand as though impelled by a catapult. I staggered back; my right arm numb to the shoulder.

The stranger bowed a third time to Edith, sheathed his sword, vaulted lightly onto his horse, and cantered out of sight down the bridle-path.

"Oh," gasped Edith, running toward me in dire fear, "you are hurt! You are wounded? Where?"

I made no reply. Instead, I bounded furiously down the path in murderous pursuit of the unknown man who had insulted, humiliated, and then outfought me.

Chapter VI.
Treason!

IT was late afternoon when I reached headquarters. General Arnold was expected back that evening. And I returned to the Robinson house ahead of the other picknickers in order to prepare some reports for him.

I had run in blind, raging pursuit of the mysterious stranger until my breath had given out. But I had caught no sight of him along the winding aisles of the woodland bridle-path. Nor had I so much as heard the distant beats of his horse's hoofs.

He had appeared between us like a ghost. He had vanished like one. There was something uncanny about it all. Who or what could he be?

That wilderness was the last sort of place where one would expect to encounter a lone stranger, in elegant civilian garb, with the manners of a Versailles aristocrat, and superhuman skill as a swordsman.

He had dropped, seemingly, from the clouds, had spoken to me as though I were a rebellious black slave, had bested me (good fencer and strong man though I was) as easily as if I were a schoolboy; and had ridden away into—*nothingness*.

Through all my baffled rage I had a feeling of unreality, a chill of apprehension at such a mystery; yet this but fanned my hate.

Never before had I hated anyone as I hated this stranger who had so readily put me in the wrong, chided me, and then put me to rout in fair fight—all in the presence of a woman.

"He took me by surprise," I muttered to myself as I sat in the library at headquarters compiling my reports. "If he had not, I should never have been disarmed by a cheap French trick of sword-play. Next time—"

I stopped and rubbed the muscles of my right arm, still aching from the wrench that had hurled my sword from my hand.

The library door swung open and Edith Bliss hurried into the room, closing it softly behind her and advancing in haste toward me. I rose, confused. Now was my chance to make the apology that the stranger's advent had cut short.

I was ashamed to meet her eye, remembering how despicably ludicrous a figure I had presented when last she had seen me.

But she gave me no time for hesitation. Her manner was one of ill-repressed excitement. Her big eyes were alight with fright.

Running up to me, she thrust into my hands a slip of folded paper.

"Read this!" she panted. "I found it but now behind the rack where the cloaks hang. It was open. It had fallen from some pocket. Since the general is not yet back, I brought it to you. You will know best what to do with it."

Wondering at her eagerness and fear, I took the folded paper. It seemed an enclosure such as might have slipped from some sheaf of documents. Its contents were brief. They were written in a grotesquely cramped, evidently disguised, hand, which withal seemed somehow not wholly unfamiliar to me:

MR. JOHN ANDERSON, *Merchant:*
W. goes to H. for a month on the date named. Tell C. that next week appears to me best time for commercial enterprise. Must have personal interview. Tell C. I stipulate for safety and release of persons named in subjoined list. Dare not trust plans of W. P. to post. You must receive them in person. Set date.
GUSTAVUS.

The stilted, disjointed screed filled me with a sudden terror that had never been mine in the fiercest battle. Under the formal language I read the sinister intent as though in letters of flame.

"W. goes to H." That was Washington, of course, who had but just lately departed for Hartford. "W. P.—West Point."

Some one familiar with all our arrangements had, then, written to notify one "John Anderson" that Washington was out of the way, and that an enterprise—against West Point, no doubt—would now be safe.

In another paper, according to the letter, was a list of persons to be spared in case of an attack. And the plans of our great fortress were to be turned over by "Gustavus" in person.

Who was "C."? Who but Sir Henry Clinton, commander of the British forces in New York?

I raised my eyes in dumb horror to Edith's. She was watching me with nervous intentness.

"I was not mistaken, then?" she cried. "I see by your face I was not. Oh, the *shame* of it! To think we have a traitor here! A man with whom we are perhaps in daily talk. A man we trust. A man who seeks to betray West Point to the enemy. I—I can't believe it."

"It cannot be doubted," I returned, dazed with the shock. "The letter is only too clear. So much for General Arnold's foolish faith in his fellow men! This letter is from some one he trusts, some one who knows the plans of West Point. A spy of the British who has wormed his way into the general's confidence."

"Can you guess, from the handwriting—"

"No. It is palpably disguised. Yet I seem to have seen it before. I wish I could think where. It must be some one on the staff; or else some one whose correspondence the general has given me to answer."

"Is there any one you suspect?"

"There is not a man in Arnold's whole army that I believe capable of such a thing. There is no date to this. It was written before his excellency left for Hartford. That is all we know. Since then—"

"Since then the traitor may well have met this 'John Anderson,'" she exclaimed. "The fortress plans may even now be in General Clinton's hands."

"Oh, if only Arnold were back! *He* would know what to do. He always knows," I groaned. "I would set out at once to meet him if only I knew which road he is to take. He will be here to-night, though. We must wait till then."

"If West Point falls, it will be our heaviest blow since we lost New York," she murmured. "Oh, if—"

"Our *'heaviest'* blow? It will be our *death* blow! West Point and its Highland forts not only give us the mastery of the upper Hudson, but, if we were to lose them, the New England Colonies would be cut off from the rest of the country, and the British could subdue each unsupported section at their leisure. The whole Revolution's fate hangs on West Point. The man who seeks to betray *that* is ten times the traitor that the betrayer of any of our other strongholds would be. His name deserves to go through the ages linked with Iscariot's. For he is bartering *liberty*."

I could scarce hold my voice steady. Forgot were my own discontent, my half-formed thoughts of mutiny. In face of this new horror I stood aghast.

"I have not spoken to any one else of this," went on Edith. "I was afraid of inadvertently warning the traitor. I wish—"

Again the library door flew open. A portly, fine-looking man limped in. His cloak and boots were dusty from long riding.

As he entered I drew myself up and saluted. For this was my commander, Major-General Benedict Arnold.

Less than forty years old, of a splendid presence that even his lameness (caused by a wound in the left leg, received at Saratoga) could not mar, the general was a figure to draw attention in any company.

He was the bravest of the brave, a born commander and strategist, a man in every sense of the word.

As a mere boy of fifteen he had run away from home to fight in the French and Indian Wars. Later, when he was a rich and respected physician of New Haven, he had thrown away wealth and home in order to serve his country.

Since the day when news came of the battles of Concord and Lexington, he had ever been foremost in the field.

George Washington was his dearest friend. And the men to whom Washington gave his full friendship were few and of high merit.

Gallant, hot-tempered, full of magnetic charm, burning with wrath at the cruelly unjust treatment accorded him by Congress, Benedict Arnold was in those days my ideal of all that was greatest and best in man.

The general glanced with amused surprise at Edith and myself as we stood close together, facing him. He uncovered and bowed to her. She courtesied and slipped from the room.

"Well, lad!" he cried playfully, "is this the way you do your work in my absence? Flirting with my son's dainty governess is far pleasanter occupation, I doubt not, than poring over musty reports."

He threw aside his cloak as he talked, and flicked at his dusty high boots with a cambric handkerchief.

"General—" I began.

He glanced quickly at me.

"Why, lad!" he cried in sudden concern. "Are you ill? You're white as a sheet. And you look fifty years old. What is amiss?"

I handed him the letter without comment.

He glanced over the single sheet with its burden of cramped handwriting. I watched him. The ruddy color ebbed from his face, leaving it haggard and gray.

His dark eyes glowed as though a fire burned behind them. His strong hand fell a-shaking, so that the paper slipped from between his stiffened fingers.

"Mistress Bliss found this abominable thing," said I, stooping to pick it up and returning it to him. "She found it but now, behind the cloak rack. Mayhap it has lain there for days. She brought it to me and—"

"Has she shown it to others?" he broke in, his voice harsh and cracked. "Has she, think you? To Madam Arnold, or to—"

"To no one. I am certain. Have you any suspicion what man—"

"Suspicion?" he roared. "Not I! If I had I would kill him with my bare hands. Have—do—do you recognize the scrawl?"

"No. Yet there is a sort of familiar look to it, as in the face of a friend when that face is distorted and swollen out of shape."

"It is none of *my* officers. Of that I make oath. Wayne, give me a pledge to speak of this to no one."

"Willingly, sir. I ask but to help you discover—"

"Not even to Mistress Bliss. Should she speak to you again of the matter, keep silence. You promise?"

"Certainly," I assented, in wonder. "But who—"

"You think she will hold her tongue? She will not babble to everybody?"

"To no one. I am sure of that."

He was pacing back and forth, up and down the library, his long, limping stride oddly like that of a stage tragedian. His handsome face was livid and twisted. His gray lips uttered incoherencies.

Never had I seen the fearless leader so utterly devoid of self-control. I sought in vain for words to console him.

Full well did I realize what this must mean to Arnold. Robbed of the honors that were rightly his, placed on trial for faults he had not committed, publicly reprimanded by Washington, wrongfully deprived of his Philadelphia command—and now in danger of losing, through treachery, the all important fortress entrusted to his care! It seemed the very climax of a life of unmerited misfortune.

"It is not yet too late," I ventured. "The British may perchance have the plans of West Point, through the treachery of one of our men. But West Point itself still stands. There are brave arms ready to defend it to the death. And the words 'Arnold' and 'Defeat' are still strangers to each other."

The general smiled wanly.

"Dear lad," he said, "you are the most loyal friend I have. And my friendship has been almost as bad a handicap to you as his excellency's has been for me. I wish for your sake my fortunes might mend."

"Yet you are in high favor just now, general. As commandant of West Point—"

"As commandant of West Point I am accountable to every scoundrel who hates me. And my ruin is but a question of time. They'll trump up new charges against me before long. I half wish I had never thrown in my lot with this hopeless revolution. If I had taken service in the British army—"

"General!"

"Pay no heed to my growls, lad. This vile news of treachery has upset me. But I have a feeling that the next few weeks may see the end of 'Arnold Ill-Luck.'"

Chapter VII.
A Night Adventure.

IT was the next morning that I saw Edith Bliss again. She sought me out to ask for further news of the treason letter and to inquire how Arnold might be setting to work to catch the traitor.

Mindful of my promise to the general, I told her nothing. I was monstrous civil this time, but coldly refused to say one word of the subject so near to her heart.

After an unanswered question or two she noticed the odd restraint and confusion in my manner. And I could see she misread it.

Her frank friendliness suddenly gave way to an equal reserve; I almost thought, to a tinge of suspicion. And she walked away, leaving me standing miserable.

Nor from Arnold could I get another word on the theme. In reply to a guarded query on my part, a day or two later, he replied curtly that he had reliable agents at work upon the case, and reiterated his order that I keep my mouth closed.

Nevertheless, to my superheated imagination the very air throbbed with secret treason. In every messmate I sought to detect a spy.

A dozen meaningless happenings I distorted as having a bearing upon the treachery. Altogether, I was in an overexcited, suspicious frame of mind, and neglected my work and my meals alike.

It is no comfortable sensation to know that among a group of your seemingly honest comrades, one is a criminal, and to wonder if perchance it is your own roommate or the man who sits next you at table.

I took to avoiding my fellows, and to spending much of my time in prowling alone about the surrounding country, pondering on the terrible secret that was mine and vainly seeking means to solve the mystery.

Once or twice, as I slunk off on such walks, I saw Edith Bliss's big, grave eyes watching me with troubled doubt. Yes, and with some other expression I could not fathom.

She kept out of my way nowadays. I had no speech with her. And this, too, vaguely set my heart to aching. I knew not why.

One evening, I was returning late from one of my solitary rambles. The moon was up, but the skies were close clouded. An elusive gray light rested over everything.

I chanced to pass near the Robinson boathouse on my way to headquarters. As I approached it I dimly saw a skiff shoot out from the little dock.

I could just make out a single shrouded figure at the rower's bench. Also, from the absence of sound, I knew the oars were muffled.

Now, who at headquarters would set forth close to midnight in silence? Also why, on so breathlessly hot a night, should the mysterious rower go wrapped in a cloak?

Instantly to my suspicious mind leaped the thought of treason. Was this the writer of the "Gustavus" letter? Was he going, perchance, to that "personal interview" his letter had demanded? The idea fired me with eagerness.

In vain I told myself the rower was probably some soldier from the West Point barracks who had overstayed his leave on the east bank of the river and was hurrying secretly back to duty.

Even as that possibility occurred to me, he shifted his course southward. Such a direction would land him far south of West Point.

I remembered then that in the afternoon I had once more seen the British sloop of war Vulture lying at anchor some miles down-stream.

Was this midnight oarsman bound for the sloop? It was certainly worth while to follow in the hope of recognizing, if not stopping, him.

Quick as thought, I ran silently down the bank toward the boathouse. I had scarce reached it when from the shadows a second rowboat darted out into the stream.

I halted in my tracks to note this new apparition. In the faint, elusive gray light, I could see the second rower was also cloaked, and that he bent to his oars with absolute noiselessness.

Yes; and more. The second boat was unquestionably following the first, and with the caution of a panther stalking its prey.

It was very evident from the second oarsman's maneuvers that he was eager to escape the observation of the first and to stick close to the latter's tracks.

Decidedly, this was well worth following up. The quick fever of the man-hunt was upon me.

I entered the boat-house, noted that but four of the six skiffs belonging there were in their slips, and stepped into the lightest of these.

I ripped off my neckcloth, tore it in two; and muffled both oarlocks. Then I pushed out into the stream.

The first boat was scarce visible in the dim light, almost wholly hidden by the low film of mist that lay over the river. The second boat was half concealed by the mist.

I ventured to follow, rowing with infinite caution, and taking good care not to approach near enough to attract notice.

Ordinarily, this would have been impossible. But the second rower was so intent on watching the first that he apparently did not trouble to safeguard against being trailed. I had merely to keep my distance and to avoid making the faintest noise.

An odd scene we must have presented, we three, each rowing silently and swiftly along in the weird gray gloom, each unaware that he was being followed.

I had lost sight of the first man, and was now forced to guide my course wholly by that of the second.

Who was the first rower? Probably the traitor. And the second? Perhaps one of the "trusted agents" Arnold had spoken of. In which case it was of course no concern of mine to join in the chase.

But two heads are better than one. And I had, moreover, a morbid hope of being able to discover something that might chance to escape the agent's vigilance.

I was Arnold's closest friend. It irked me and surprised me that he should choose other persons than myself when such a desperate venture was afoot.

I longed to outdo the agent in the matter of discovering who the traitor might be.

It is an eery sensation to row alone at midnight over a quiet, misty river. It is doubly so when one is following out a quest, like mine. Where and how the chase would end I could not guess.

I wished I had chanced to be wearing my sword or carried a pistol. I was quite unarmed. And it was not likely that either of the men I pursued was in similarly defenseless state.

Yet, I counted on my mighty strength, if it should come to a question of violence. And, besides, was I not fighting for liberty?

The row was longer than I had expected. Southwesterly we moved. I seemed to have been tugging at the oars for an eternity.

Once or twice I lost sight of the second boat, but ever found it again.

At last I neared the west bank of the Hudson, some miles south of West Point. The skiff I was following ran in among the shadows of the woods that sloped down to the very beach.

I stopped rowing. Then, faintly, I heard the grating of a keel upon the shore-gravel. And I knew my quarry had landed.

For a full minute longer I remained motionless, to give him time to tie his boat and climb the bank. Then softly I rowed ashore and brought my skiff to a standstill close beside his.

The first man's boat I could see nowhere. Nor did I trouble to look for it. The second was doubtless hard upon its track.

My present task, then, was to follow the second man, knowing full well he would soon or late guide me unconsciously to the first.

I only hoped he would not scare his prey prematurely and turn him from his mission. I wanted the scoundrel to be caught red-handed.

I had had no possible means of identifying either of the oarsmen. Not only was the light bad, but both had been too far away from me and too completely hidden in their big cloaks.

Up the wooded bank I stole, moving soundlessly as any Iroquois. I reached the top, and could just make out a narrow, twisted path running inland.

Along this, probably, the two men—pursuer and pursued—had just passed. If not, I dared not risk noise by crashing through the adjacent undergrowth trying to pick up their trail.

The path seemed the only probable clue to my vanished quarry. And along the path I cautiously started.

For two or three minutes I walked. Then, just ahead of me, I saw an opening in the trees. I reached it and found I was at one end of a wide glade. At first glance I could see no one.

Then, as I stepped forward, sick at heart with the fear that I had lost the trail, I managed to discern two shadowy figures, perhaps a hundred feet ahead of me.

Crouching low, and taking advantage of each bush and rock, I crept toward them. Presently I could catch the sibilant sound of whispers.

I could see the two shapes a little more clearly than before. One of the two—the shorter—was evidently the rower of the first or second boat, and still wore the enshrouding cloak.

The second, however, did not seem to be one of the oarsmen. He wore no cloak, and had not the general appearance of either of the persons I had been following.

Again stooping over, I stole forward, until I was a bare twenty feet from them. I had noticed for some moments that the night had grown lighter. Now, all at once, the full moon tore its way through the mass of scudding clouds, making everything in the glade dazzlingly bright.

I sprang to my full height. The cloaked figure quickly turned as a twig snapped under my foot. Then I halted in crass amaze.

It was Edith Bliss!

Edith Bliss here, at this hour of night. A sting of jealousy shot through me. I shifted my bewildering gaze on the man beside her.

Then the moonlight falling full on his face, I knew who it was.

Something seemed to snap in my brain. With a half animal snarl I sprang at him.

Chapter VIII.
I Meet Mine Enemy.

FOR the man who stood talking alone to Edith Bliss in the moonlit glade was the stranger who had disarmed and shamed me a week before—the man I had vowed to punish at risk of my own life.

And now my long-nursed hatred for him was redoubled by a wild surge of some emotion I instinctively knew for jealousy.

Yet, that same onrush of jealousy also brought me sanity. I was unarmed. I could not further lower myself in Edith's eyes by a hand-to-hand rough-and-tumble fight in her presence.

I must bear myself as much a polished man of the world as was my unknown enemy.

Were I to play the brute before his eyes, I should still further emphasize the difference between his deadly courtesy and my own boorishness. The thought checked me.

I halted in my savage forward rush ere either of them had guessed my murderous intent. I halted, I say, then moved forward with erect shoulders and dignified step, casting off my light cloak and doffing my hat.

Approaching the stranger, I bowed to him in stiff, formal greeting. With a faint start of wonder, he returned my salute (far more gracefully than I could have bowed had I practised before a pier-glass for weeks).

Ere he could speak, I turned to Edith, who shrank back from me, her great eyes dilated with a strange horror.

"Mistress Bliss," quoth I, monstrous polite, "I ask forgiveness for so sudden an interruption of your pleasant chat. But may I entreat you to withdraw? I have pressing, urgent business with this—gentleman, business that brooks no instant of delay."

Now, even in such moment of stress, I rather prided myself on that little speech of mine. It seemed to fulfil every requirement both of need and courtesy.

Instead of blindly attacking the fellow, and subjecting a delicate girl to the spectacle of a brutal hand-to-hand combat, I had most suavely besought her to move away, leaving the stranger and myself to settle our stern account untrammeled by witnesses, unvexed by feminine shrieks of fear.

Yet the effect of my formal words was quite astounding. To my horror, the girl burst into a sudden passion of weeping. With an impulsive little cry, she ran forward and caught me by the arm with both her white hands.

"Oh!" she moaned. "'Tis as feared, then! And I hoped—yes, and *prayed*—that I might be wrong. That you, bravest of our post officers, should sink to this! Oh, the *shame* of it! The *cruel* shame!"

"'Should *sink* to this!'" I echoed, dumfounded. "I see no matter of 'shame.' I have sought for days the opportunity to meet this man. He wears a sword; I do not. Yet I am prepared to waive that advantage. I fail to see what shame I incur by meeting, face to face—"

She did not understand. She did not even hear. She was wailing again in piteous appeal:

"The shame of it! And I so looked up to you and honored you and sought your friendship! Forego this vile thing you mean to do! For *my* sake. For your country's sake. For the holy sake of *liberty*. Can you recall Washington's noble face, and then do the unspeakable thing you came here to do?"

Now, little by little, through the murk of surprise, I thought I began to see light. It was her mention of Washington that gave me what seemed a clue.

I recalled that his excellency had but recently issued an edict forbidding his officers to fight duels, and reminding them that their lives were too precious to their country to be thrown away in idle personal quarrels.

Doubtless, then, Edith knew I meant to fight the stranger, and was seeking to turn me from my purpose. Yet I wondered that she, who was usually so gay and self-controlled, should now be weeping hysterically, and beseeching me in the name of liberty to desist from my purpose.

She had shown far less emotion, a week agone, when she had beheld the stranger and myself actually crossing swords.

I could not understand her agony of entreaty, her panic-terror. Had she and the stranger met frequently, perchance, during these past seven days?

And had she in that time learned to care so dearly for him that the thought of his suffering possible hurt at my hands was unbearable to her?

This seemed the one solution. All at once I felt it *was* the solution. Her tears, her heartbroken entreaties, were for him! At the thought a white-hot pain rent my heart, and my brain reeled.

In that moment of blinding, agonizing mental light, I knew I loved Edith Bliss.

I loved her—yes, as I had never dreamed man could love. And she—she loved the stranger!

It may be my logic was poor, that I jumped over-hastily at conclusions. But show me the ardent, despairing lover who can argue with clear correctness, and I will show you the eighth wonder of the world. I looked down into her tear-stained, terror-stricken little face, so white and hopeless as the pallid moonlight fell upon it. And, as I looked, a mighty wave of pity engulfed me.

She loved him. She was pleading with me for his life. And my own hopeless adoration led me to the first real sacrifice I had ever made.

For her sake, I would spare this lover of hers. I would forego my cherished revenge.

She must have seen the softening in my face, for she cried, with a tinge of hope in her sweet, trembling voice:

"You will not do it? You will give up this wicked plan? Oh, I knew you would. I was sure I had not so utterly misjudged you. I understand it all. You think you have been ill-used. You have brooded over your misfortune and your delayed hopes until this terrible thing you were about to do seemed almost right to you. I thank Heaven I followed you to-night and arrived in time to save you from deathless ignominy.

"Now you will have no dealing with this man? You will come back with me? Back to the duty you have always performed so splendidly. Back to the brother officers who love and trust you, whose love and respect you would forever have forfeited. No one shall know the truth from me. We will both forget it. It shall be as if the temptation had never come to you!"

Faith! The girl was talking like any parson. Had I come hither meditating some low crime, instead of for natural vengeance upon mine enemy, she could not have been more eloquent, more wildly grateful at having won me over.

Through all my misery I could almost have smiled at her idea that a fair duel would have forfeited whatever kindly feeling my rough military comrades might have had for me.

Nowadays the duel is falling into disrepute, and rightly so; but in the days whereof I speak (full thirty years ago), it was deemed no part of a brave man's duty to refrain from single combat in defense of his honor.

"You will give up this temptation?" she said again as I hesitated.

"Yes," I made answer. "For your sake. Not for that of my country, for I do not admit that my country has the right to demand such a thing of me. But if it will add to your own peace of mind, I give you my sacred promise not to carry out my intent."

She drew a long, shivering sigh of relief, and made as though to speak. Then, attracted by the sound of a footstep crossing the glade, she paused, glanced keenly in the direction of the sound, then drew back with a sharp intake of breath.

I turned to see what it was that had so surprised her. Crossing the glade toward us came a cloaked man. He was still more than fifty yards away.

Yet, from his limp, I knew him. It was Benedict Arnold. We three, standing in the shadow of the woodland's edge, were still invisible to the advancing newcomer.

I glanced from him to where Edith Bliss had stood a moment before. She had vanished. Doubtless, thought I, she, too, recognized Arnold, and did not wish to explain to her employer her presence there at such an hour of night.

So it was that, the moment or so before the general reached us, the stranger and I stood alone together.

"Surely," he said in a low voice, "it was *you* whom I was to meet here to-night? I cannot have mistaken the hour and the place. You were sent here to meet me by—"

Arnold caught sight of our forms and stood still. The stranger, noting the general's pause, broke off his sentence and asked me with some slight apprehension:

"This is one of your men?"

"No," I made reply. "It is General Benedict Arnold."

"Ah!" he exclaimed with satisfaction. "All is well, then. I fancied, being detained, he had sent you in his place. I have not met him before: Pray introduce me."

Wondering, I followed, as he stepped briskly forward toward the general. Why should Arnold appoint this lonely midnight meeting with any man? It was all beyond me.

Yet I made shift to range myself alongside the stranger. We halted as we stood in front of Arnold, and I said:

"General, permit me to present to you Mr.—Mr.—"

"Mr. John Anderson," supplemented the stranger, bowing.

The name was scarce past his lips when, with a tiger spring, I was at his throat and had borne the man to earth.

Chapter IX.
A Strange Vigil.

"AND, general," I cried, exultant, pinioning the writhing man to the ground by main force, "permit me to present to you, for hanging, the fellow with whom the unknown traitor at West Point is corresponding. We have the clue to the foul mystery at last, right here under my hands. Shall I save the hangman the trouble of strangling him, or would you question him first?"

I was athrill with savage joy. For Edith's sake I had been willing to spare her lover as long as that lover was merely my personal enemy.

But now that I knew him for the "Mr. John Anderson" to whom

the mysterious "Gustavus" had written to barter our liberty, all the love in the world could not have held me back from his throat.

"General," I cried again, while Arnold still stood watching our struggling forms with sheer numbness of amazement, "this man spoke but now of coming here to-night to meet you. He lied, of course, to hide the fact that he was to meet the 'Gustavus.' I will gag and bind him, and then you and I will wait in the shadows to welcome Gustavus on his arrival. 'Twill be rare sport, and the treason will die unhatched. We—"

I got no further. Arnold, with a savage cry, had seized my shoulders and was tugging me away from my victim.

Strong man as the general was, he could not have budged me one inch but for the fact that he was my commander.

"You young fool!" Arnold shouted. "Let him up! Let him up, I say! You well-nigh killed him. What means this ruffianly behavior?"

I got to my feet and stared agape at him.

"General," I panted, "you don't understand. This is John Anderson, the spy whom—"

"The *spy?*" laughed Arnold heartily, his flash of rage giving way to noisy mirth. "Man, this is John Anderson, one of my most faithful agents—a man who even now is on a mission of life and death import for me! And you tried to kill him. Have you *no* wits?"

Sheepishly, still angry, wholly baffled and confused, I looked on dumbly while the general helped the discomfited Anderson to rise, and brushed from his clothes the forest mold and leaves.

Anderson, rearranging his twisted neckcloth, looked from one to the other of us in careless indifference. Even then I admired the splendid coolness of the man.

"General Arnold," I said in a last effort, "I showed you last week a letter from some unknown man in our army offering to sell Clinton the plans of West Point. The letter was addressed to one John Anderson. I find this man here, at midnight, awaiting some one. And—"

"And it is *I* he was awaiting," rapped out Arnold. "We meet here by appointment, because the very secrecy of his mission forbids his being seen at headquarters. He is an officer of note, and is supposed to be even now with Gates's army. If it were known he is in this neighborhood, everything would be lost. Your crazy over-zeal came nigh to ruining all."

"But he is *Anderson*—John Anderson. He—"

"Lad," said Arnold impatiently, "there are three million people in the thirteen Colonies, and out of that number, I doubt not, no less than a hundred are named John Anderson. Did it never occur to you that a spy and an honest man might both chance to bear the same very common name? Why, 'John Anderson' is well-nigh as oft heard as 'John Smith.' If you should meet a John Smith, would you fall on your knees before him in veneration under the impression he might be the Captain John Smith who settled Virginia in 1609? Nonsense! Have five years of campaigning taught you nothing, that you must fly at a man's throat like—"

"But," I broke in all at once, scanning the stranger more closely in the moonlight, "look! I had not noted before. He is in the uniform of a British major. He—"

"To be sure he is," sighed Arnold, with the air of one teaching a lesson to a very simple child. "To be sure, he is in British uniform, at my orders. He goes to New York for me at dawn. Would you have him walk into the British barracks there dressed in his own uniform of an American captain?"

A spy. But one of our own.

I began to see. The stranger was going to New York—into the very jaws of the British lion—on secret service work for our cause, even as gallant Nathan Hale had gone.

To insure secrecy, Arnold had planned to meet him in this very desolate place for final instructions, lest some traitor at headquarters— "Gustavus," perhaps—might betray his identity to the British.

Anderson was going to risk his life among the enemy, at Arnold's orders and in behalf of liberty. And I, idiot that I was, had sought to destroy the whole scheme. I could have groaned aloud for sheer chagrin at my own rash senselessness.

General Arnold was ever a keen reader of men. He read my face now like an open book.

"There, there, lad!" he said kindly. "Take it not so hard. You meant it all for the best."

"Failure's path is strewn with the bones of those who 'meant it all for the best,'" I muttered in angry self-contempt. "Captain Anderson,

I ask your pardon for my uncouth, childish behavior."

Anderson held out his hand with a charming smile. But for that smile, I doubt if I could have brought myself to shake hands with him.

For what I had just learned in no way altered the fact that he was the man Edith Bliss loved, nor that he had rebuked and then disarmed me when we had met a week since on the "neutral ground."

Yes, I realized he was a hero; a braver man than I (for a spy ever takes far more terrible risks than does the soldier who fights in open field); yet I could not banish my ill-feeling toward him.

However, we shook hands with outward courtesy, Arnold looking on with a smile. Then, with a start of displeased recollection, the general inquired:

"By the way, Phil, how do *you* chance to be here? I thought you asleep in bed at headquarters. What odd chance led you to this glade to-night?"

"I saw a skiff put out from the Robinson boat-house an hour or more ago," said I; "a cloaked figure was in it. I—"

"The mysterious cloaked figure was mine," he retorted. "And so you followed me, eh? Like any Mohican? And, losing sight of me, on this side of the river, blundered upon Anderson. I see."

I was on the point of saying that Edith Bliss had followed him across the river even more closely than had I. But, without giving me time to speak, he went on more abruptly:

"Of course you understand the absolute need of secrecy. You will not speak of this meeting. And, now that you are here, I may as well make use of you. You see that rocky knoll up yonder, overlooking the river? Stand there, on guard, till Anderson and I come to you. It commands a view of the river, both north and south. The moon is so bright now, you will be able to see any boat that draws near shore, or any one coming toward this glade by land. Anderson and I have much to say to each other, and he must be off in another hour. To your post, lad!"

I saluted and tramped off through the undergrowth, leaving the two together. I glanced back once. They were crossing the glade side by side, headed westward.

I worried at sight of this. For, a little inland, were the houses of several Tories.

What if some sleepless Tory householder should chance to be

roaming abroad and should overhear them?

The night was dead still. To my slightly nervous mind it seemed peopled with fantastic moving shadows. Once or twice I mistook bush, boulder, or shrub for a lurking foe.

Also, when I looked backward toward Arnold and Anderson, it seemed for a moment as if some half-formed shadow were stealing noiselessly along the glade in their wake. I looked more closely, but could not see the fantastic, silent shape again.

Ascribing the thing to a trick of moonlight and cloud, I hastened onward toward the knoll.

I was at first half-minded to hurry back and make sure I had not been mistaken about the flitting shadow. But I had already made a fool of myself quite often enough for one night, and I was not anxious to risk further rebuke from Arnold.

I toiled up the steep little rocky slope of the knoll, and gained the summit. Then, sitting on the highest, dew-drenched pinnacle of mossy stone, I began my vigil.

Below me, in front, lay the wide, moon-silvered ribbon of river. Behind and to each side were the black woods and paler meadowland.

To southward, a few miles, I could make out the dim bulk and spars of the British sloop of war Vulture, as she lay at anchor in mid-stream. And again I fell to wondering why a British warship should be taking these seemingly aimless excursions up the Hudson.

A single vessel could hope to make no headway against our forts; and our outposts reported no sister ships behind her.

No other craft was visible on so much of the river as I could see. My heart smote me at thought of the long, lonely, homeward row that Edith Bliss must even now be having.

I strained my eyes for sight of her bobbing skiff. But the moonlight's play on the shifting waters dazzled me, and I could not make out the boat.

I was in love. I knew it now. Not with capricious Dorothy Cary, who had played fast and loose with me for months, and had at last set me an impossible ordeal.

I knew now that my infatuation for Mistress Cary had been bred of those two inveterate matchmakers, Vanity and Propinquity, and of nothing else.

I loved Edith Bliss with all the force of my whole nature. And she not only loved another man, but loved him with a devotion that had made her plead with frantic weeping that I would spare his life.

And mentally, I added one more link to my endless chain of ill-luck.

A flash of red light from a point of land far down on the opposite bank of the river brought me back to reality. A second or two later I heard a low, rumbling roar.

I was on my feet in an instant, tense, staring.

Again, the next minute, came that flash, and again the far boom. By this time my knowledge of Hudson geography had enabled me to locate the disturbance.

It came from Teller's Point (they call it Croton Point in this nine-teenth-century of ours), on the east shore of the river. And, as any soldier would have known at once, the flash and report were from a cannon.

I saw new lights spring up here and there aboard the Vulture. The crew were awake and stirring. Lanterns, carried evidently by running men, moved fast about the deck. I could see a shadowy sail hoisted.

A third cannon-shot, then a fourth. I could now hear the distant creak of a windlass. The Vulture was lifting anchor.

I guessed correctly the meaning of the excitement on board. Some ardent patriots, seeing the Vulture lying there, had dragged a cannon into position on the water-edge at Teller's Point, and were blazing away at the anchored war-sloop.

Some of the shots, too, must have come uncomfortably close to their mark, for the Vulture was preparing to get out of range with all possible speed.

Sails set and anchor up, the British vessel swung slowly down stream as a fifth shot flashed out from the darkness of the eastern shore. A sixth was fired soon after.

The war-sloop, wafted by the light September breeze, crawled southward, and presently was lost to sight behind the nearest head-land.

So intent I had been in watching the amateur bombardment (a bit of seemingly futile patriotism, by the way, which indirectly saved our nation from destruction), that I did not hear the quick footsteps behind me until those steps were close at my heels.

Then, belatedly aware of my duty as guard, I turned with a jump to confront the intruder upon my vigil.

"Halt!" I commanded, even as I wheeled about. "Halt! Who goes?"

Chapter X.
The Man from Nowhere.

EVEN as I voiced the challenge, I recognized the newcomer. It was Arnold. He had toiled up the steep incline and stood beside me. Anderson was just below him.

"I heard cannon-shots," said the general uneasily. "What does it mean? Who at West Point can be firing, without orders, at this time of night?"

"It is not at West Point, sir," I answered, "but at Teller's Point, miles below."

"At Teller's Point? Why?"

"Some soldiers or farmers trained one of the cannon there upon the Vulture, and drove her from her moorings."

"*What?*"

He fairly screamed the word. He shook like a man in a palsy, and scanned the moonlit river everywhere for a glimpse of the British vessel.

"She sailed southward, out of sight," I told him, wondering at his unwonted violence.

While Benedict Arnold was an ideal soldier, he was no stiff-necked martinet, and I could not understand why the mere fact of a handful of patriots opening unauthorized bombardment on a hostile ship should so excite him.

My surprise was still greater when, as I told of the war-sloop's dis-appearance, he burst into the most horrible rage I had ever witnessed.

The man seemed possessed by a demon. He cursed, shrieked, raved, shook his fist at the smiling skies, and denounced everything between heaven and earth.

I stood aghast. Not even when he was arraigned by Congress on false charges, at Philadelphia—not when Ethan Allen took from him the glory of the Ticonderoga campaign—not when Gates stole from him the reward for the victory at Saratoga—had I seen him half so moved.

"The fates themselves war against me," he railed at last, as his revilings grew more coherent. "Man and destiny have ever conspired to thwart my dearest hopes. But I will beat them yet! I will conquer in spite of everything! Like Samson, I will tear down the whole structure they have reared, and crush them all beneath it."

Now, this seemed to me utterly babyish language for a grown man to use, just because a few harmless cannon-shots had been fired without his orders. I realized that he must be under terrific stress of nervous emotion if so trivial an incident could cause him such fury.

Then, remembering what the mysterious treachery at West Point must mean to him, and how his loyal spirit must writhe under the knowledge that he had a traitor in his garrison, I straightway began to find excuses for his present lack of self-control.

When a man carries the fate of a nation in his hands, it is but natural that his nerves should sometimes show the wear and tear of over-responsibility.

Presently the general grew calmer. He glanced sideways at me, as if ashamed of his outburst.

"Wait here!" he ordered.

Then he limped down the slope, spoke a few hurried, whispered words to Anderson, and together they disappeared in the gloom.

For more than half an hour I remained at my lonely post. I inferred that the noise of the cannon had disturbed them in the midst of their talk, and that, having come to learn the cause, they had returned to finish the conference.

At last they came back to me. As they drew near my rock, Arnold called to me to climb down to them. It was then that I noticed with some astonishment Anderson no longer wore his uniform of a British major.

He was dressed in a plain riding-suit, and his white silk stockings were hidden under high boots.

I had no time to do more than glance at the man, and to wonder where and how he had secured such complete change of apparel at that hour of night, when Arnold addressed me.

"Lad," said he, speaking in the pleasant, familiar fashion that was so great a part of his charm, "I've work for you. I had planned that Anderson should dress as an English officer and be provided with papers that would let him board the Vulture without suspicion, and be carried thus to New York. Those fools over on Teller's Point, with their noisy popgun, have scared off the Vulture and upset all my arrangements."

Now I understood why he had been so angry, and I found far more excuse for his gust of rage.

"Therefore," went on the general, "I have had to recast my scheme. Anderson has put on civilian dress. He will cross the river and ride down to New York, along the east bank, taking his chances of getting past the British sentinel line at Harlem. I shall want your help. I have just written him a pass that will let him through our army in case our outposts should try to stop him. I want you to go along as far as Ferguson's Farms. After that, the way is clear, and he can travel alone."

I saluted with no good grace. I scarce relished the idea of having for several hours the companionship of this successful rival of mine.

"Get into your boat," went on Arnold. "Row across the river as if you were pulling in a race. Go to headquarters. Saddle a couple of good horses, and bring them down to the road above the boat-house. Anderson and I will be waiting there for you. Don't awaken a trooper to do the saddling for you. Do it yourself. I want no one to know. And get the horse away without disturbing any one. Much depends on secrecy. More than you can realize. Now, go!"

I made my way to the shore; they following more slowly, and still talking earnestly in low tones. My boat was where I had left it tied. But Edith's, which had lain close beside it, was gone.

I pushed off and bent to my oars with all the strength I had, sending the light craft spinning over the still water. I recalled with grim amusement my stealthy, slow progress across, an hour or so earlier, when I had been dogging Edith's boat and she Arnold's.

What a mare's nest the "mystery" had proved itself! By the light of later events, I could so readily piece together the whole fabric.

Edith (probably approaching the boat-house in order to cross the Hudson and keep her tryst with Anderson) had seen Arnold putting off from shore. Mistaking him, perhaps, for me, and with her mind full of the treason plot, she had followed. Then I, seeing her, and being also full of the manhunt craze, had given chase. How absurd it was!

I passed an empty, floating skiff. I hardly glanced at it. It was not capsized. The water was too calm for any one to have been upset. I supposed the boat had been left unfastened and had drifted away.

In much less time than I had come to the west bank I made the long return trip to the boat-house, then ran at top speed to headquarters.

Moving noiselessly, I managed to saddle and lead out two of the fastest horses in the officers' stable without awakening any one.

Giving the countersign for the night, I led them past the wondering sentry at the gate, and so on down the half-mile road leading to the boat-house.

There I found Arnold and Anderson, who had just landed and were coming toward me.

Anderson vaulted to the saddle of one of the two horses with the grace of a dancing master, adjusted his stirrups, and turned his mount's head southward. I followed his example.

Arnold reached up and grasped my hand in good-by. I noted that his own was clammy and cold. Then he turned to Anderson.

The latter, to my surprise, evidently failed to notice the general's outstretched hand, but saluted and set off at a canter. I urged my own steed to a gallop and caught up with him.

"General Arnold," I remarked, "offered to shake hands with you."

"Did he?" queried Anderson dryly.

I did not know what reply to make, and for a space we rode on without speaking. I had no wish to follow up the conversation. It was ordeal enough to be forced to ride at all with this man who had bested me in manners and in swordsmanship, and who had won the heart of the girl I loved.

In the saddle, with the night breeze in one's face, the moon above and a good horse beneath, it is hard to remain glum. Sad at heart though I was, I yet caught myself indulging unconsciously in an old habit of mine when on long, lonely rides. Namely, of humming a song under my breath.

I did not realize what I was singing, nor, indeed, that I was singing at all. Yet, to the air of "Yankee Doodle," I found myself at the last verse of a song that had caused some merriment at headquarters that season.

It was called "The Cow Chase." Written by a clever young English officer, it satirized "Mad Anthony" Wayne's famous raids on the British cattle. The final stanza ran:

> "And now I close my epic strain.
>   I tremble as I show it,
> Lest that same warrior-drover, Wayne,
>   Should ever catch the poet."

John Anderson's amused laugh broke in upon my muttered singing.

"So that doggerel has traveled as far as West Point, eh?" my companion queried.

"'Tis not doggerel," I contradicted. "'Tis a vastly amusing song, even though a Briton did write it."

"So?" he asked. "An Englishman was the author? That is of interest."

"A young British major on service under Clinton," I answered, momentarily thawed out of my reserve by the very common failing— a desire to give information. "He was the author. John André is his name. The cleverest, most reckless Englishman in all the Colonies, so I am told. 'Mad Anthony' laughed as hard at the song as any of the rest of us."

"Major John André?" repeated Anderson. "The name seems, somehow, familiar. You know him, perhaps?"

"I have never seen him," said I. "And I am not likely to, unless on field of battle. I am sorry. For they say he is a man of rare wit and good looks. And a gentleman to boot."

"Pah!" laughed Anderson. "I had heard otherwise. A great, loutish fellow, I am told, with a stable-boy's manners."

"You are wrong," I corrected him with some heat. "My information comes first-hand. From General Dale, of Washington's own staff."

"Dale? You mean the Ralph Dale who was once a spy?"

"Yes, and before that an actor. He left the stage to join the army. His wit and his powers of disguise made him of use to Washington as a spy. He entered Philadelphia on secret service while the British were in possession. It was during the Valley Forge winter. At Philadelphia he fell in love with the Hon. Miriam Dacre—the same who is now his wife. He—"

"I have met her," chimed in Anderson. "A glorious girl. And she married Dale, did she?"

"The next spring. But that is not part of my story about André. Dale escaped from Philadelphia by Mistress Dacre's aid. Later he heard false news that the British were to hang her for helping him get free. Back he rushed to Philadelphia to offer his life for hers. To this Major John André he went with his proposition. From him he learned Mistress Dacre was in no peril."

"And André had the Yankee spy neatly trapped?"

"Quite so. Yet, André did not look at it in that way. He deemed that a man who would risk life for love was too good to be hanged as a spy. So he set him free. Dale told me the tale himself. Said André: 'If I do wrong in letting an enemy escape like this, may I myself hang as a spy!' So gallant an Englishman would be well worth meeting."

Anderson yawned behind his hand. It was plain my narrative did not greatly interest him. Yet he roused himself to polite attention.

"I, too, am a spy," said he a little sadly, "though a month ago I would have challenged the man who dared say I should become one. So I should have a kindly feeling for this André of yours. Perhaps I may meet him in New York."

"I envy you the prospect," I replied. "But if you mingle with the officers there, you are certain to run across him. I am told he is ever the center of all that is gayest and brightest. The 'life of the whole garrison,' they call him."

"Ah? A buffoon? A sort of Merry Andrew? A garrison jester? It is a type for which I care little."

"You wrong him," I declared. "If he is the life of the place, it is because of his magnetism, his great heart, and his wondrous manner. And that same heart of his, if reports do not lie, carries a wound of its own. He was betrothed, in England, I hear, to a Mistress Honoria Sneyd. Her parents forbade the match. And André came hither to the war that he might win a fame which would soften their hearts. 'Tis said he ever wears her miniature in a locket about his neck."

I paused. In the moonlight I could see that Anderson's face had suddenly changed. There was a look of pain in his handsome eyes.

I knew the subject I had hit upon was distasteful to him. And I could well guess why.

Was he not also riding to danger—perhaps to a spy's shameful death—and leaving behind a girl who loved him.

Little as I liked the man, I was angry at my own lack of tact.

But, even as I checked my speech, the sad look was gone from his face. He turned toward me with the most winning smile I have ever seen, and, to banish my memory of his melancholy, launched forth into a flood of gay talk.

His cleverness, his magnetic manner, his fund of information and brilliant way of expressing himself all held me spellbound. For more than an hour we rode thus, chatting like brothers; while I felt myself more and more drawn toward my wholly delightful companion.

Seldom has time passed so rapidly. His stories of men and of events, his quick wit, his infectious laugh, were a revelation to me. I sat entranced, like one at a play, doing little more than to answer when he questioned, content to listen and to enjoy.

Dawn had broken when we came to Ferguson's Farms, where we must part. We halted our horses. And our hands met in a hearty farewell grip of friendship.

"Godspeed!" he cried as he galloped away to the southward.

I looked after him until he vanished around a bend in the road. Then I turned north, and started on my lonely return ride toward headquarters.

And, as I rode, I came slowly out of the almost mesmeric state into which Anderson's talk had thrown me. I gradually recalled that this fascinating stranger with whom I had just parted on such warmly friendly terms was one and the same man as the fellow whose punishment I had vowed, and who had won Edith Bliss's love.

I had begun our ride hating him. I had ended that ride in genuine sorrow that we must part. I could not account for my own utterly illogical change of ideas.

But this much I knew: even by recalling my former humiliation at Anderson's hands and the fact that Edith loved him, I could not work myself back into my former bitter dislike for him.

I could, and did, however, manage to feel a very wholesome contempt for my own fickleness of nature, and a real wonder that I, who was usually so slow to form friendships, should have been so quickly won over by anybody.

The road was a winding one. Ahead of me, as I jogged along, I heard the *thud-thud-thud* of galloping hoofs. Some one was coming toward me from the north—perhaps from headquarters—in mad haste.

I was enough of a horseman to realize that the steed whose flying hoof-beats grew momentarily closer to me was being ridden with unmerciful speed.

I checked my own horse and drew to one side of the road. Around the curve in front of me swept the furiously running horse.

At sight of the rider I cried aloud in amazement.

Chapter XI.
I Ride On Double Quest.

THE rider was Edith Bliss.

Bareheaded, clad in the white house-gown she had worn the preceding evening, she was urging forward one of our cavalry chargers. She had thrown one stirrup over the pommel, converting the back covering into a rude side-saddle.

With gold hair flying loose, her big pansy eyes glowing from a dead white face, she came around the curve. In the belt of her gown— oddly incongruous sight—a pistol was stuck.

Her horse, leaning to one side to overcome the unbalancing effects of rounding a corner at such a pace, struck one of his fore feet against a big bit of round stone. The stone turned under his hoof, throwing the brute out of his stride.

He stumbled, plunged forward, and was saved from rolling heels over head only by the skill and strength of his rider.

How the girl kept her seat in the unaccustomed army-saddle I do not yet understand. But somehow she did it; and saved herself and her mount from a breakneck fall.

As it was, the horse, floundering to his feet, pulled up dead lame. The stumble had wrenched some leg sinew, and he could scarce move faster than a walk.

Edith, seeing his plight, drew him back and slipped to the ground. She looked about her in a hopeless despair that went straight to my heart.

It was at that moment she first caught sight of me, as I spurred forward to her assistance.

"Captain Wayne!" she cried on the instant. "Turn! Follow Mr. Anderson, and bring him back! Bring him back! Make him come."

Again I understood. Her lover had departed on this desperate life or death mission without having chance for one word of farewell with her. She could not let him go into peril without a good-by, without a kiss, a prayer for his safety.

She had learned of his departure probably from Arnold himself; had sprung on a horse and had followed.

Even though my heart gave a twinge of pain that I of all men should be chosen to bring the two together, I turned my horse as she spoke the first words. Striking spur to his side, I galloped him back over the southward road.

If love had come to me too late, it had at least brought its holy lesson of sympathy. By rapid riding I might easily overhaul Anderson.

From my knowledge of lovers, I knew how more than willing he would be to delay his journey for an hour in order to say good-by to his sweetheart.

"I'll bring him back to you!" I shouted over my shoulder. "Wait there for me."

She called something to me in an insistent, frantic tone. I could not catch its real import.

And as I could be of greater service to her by speed than by halting to hear some reiteration of her command, I did not check my gallop.

The sun was rising. The sun of a day ever to be remembered in American history. I rode at top speed, looking neither to right nor left. At that pace I should catch up with Anderson in fifteen minutes at most.

I tried to be glad that so handsome and attractive a man was to be summoned back to the side of the girl to whom he was betrothed.

I tried to be glad that I should be the means of changing that white, drawn look of Edith's to one of joy.

But I failed miserably in both mental efforts.

I fell to conjuring to mind that awful, set expression in her child-like eyes; to wondering why she should have set out on a ride with a pistol stuck in her belt.

How she must love him to go alone through that neutral ground in search of him! The neutral ground that was often infested by the worst class of blackguards from both armies.

I had passed the spot when I had parted from Anderson. I was nearing the heights to the north of Tarrytown.

A few rods farther, and I saw a group of four men standing in the center of the white road.

All four were on foot. At one side grazed a horse which I recognized first. It was the regimental charger that Anderson had ridden. Then I saw Anderson himself. Bareheaded, coatless, in stocking feet, he stood in mid-road, surrounded by three roughly dressed fellows whom at a glance I mistook for footpads.

I fancied he had been stopped and robbed by a trio of these gentry, who were often to be met with along the neutral ground. Unarmed though I was, I rushed to his rescue.

At sound of my approach all four turned. And I recognized the foremost of the three captors as Isaac Van Wart, a militiaman who had once served as my orderly.

Then I noted that his two companions were also in rough militia uniform.

"Van Wart!" I cried, reining in my horse. "What does this mean? How dare you halt an officer of our army?"

"Officer of our army?" retorted Van Wart. "This man's a spy. A dirty British spy."

"Wayne," broke in Anderson, "cannot you convince these honest fellows of my identity and make them let me ride on? You know how important is my mission."

"Of course I can," I answered, noting with wonder how deadly pale his smiling face had grown. "Let him pass, boys. I'll vouch for him."

"Can't do it, cap'n," answered Van Wart. "I'm sorry, but this looks like an ugly business. And we're responsible for him. If we let a spy pass on to New York, we're liable to get—"

"A spy!" I retorted wrathfully. "You blockhead, this is John Anderson, an officer in our own army. He is riding on special service for General Arnold."

"That's what he tells you," replied Van Wart, unmoved. "But it's a lie, all the same. How he bamboozled you into believing it I don't know."

"I showed them my passport from General Arnold," put in Anderson. "But—"

"But you tried to bribe us to let you go on," snapped a second militiaman; "and no honest officer would do that. In the first place, no officer in our down-at-heel army would be rich enough to have the handful of gold guineas you held out to us."

"That's so," said the third. "The bribe alone would prove it. If he was an officer, all he'd need to do would be to show us the general's pass, and he could have gone on his way. It's my belief that pass is forged."

"It is not," I replied. "I saw the general give it to him."

I could see they did not believe me. Van Wart stepped up to my horse's side and told his story.

"It's this way, cap'n," he began. "Me and Paulding and Williams here was sitting at the side of the road over a little game of cards. Along canters this Anderson. He stops and asks us the way. We ask where he's going. He takes us for a British outpost, I guess. For he answers: 'To New York.' And then I says: 'What party do you belong to?' And he answers: 'To the Lower Party, of course; just as you lads do.' Then Paulding grabs his horse's rein and—"

"And," added Paulding, "he goes white and mutters something about making a mistake, and he pulls out this big gold watch and a lot of gold pieces and offers them to us to set him free. We hauled him off his horse and searched him. Van Wart found a sheaf of papers stuck away inside one of his boots."

"Papers?" I cried. "What was in them?"

"That's telling!" returned Van Wart, wagging his head wisely. "I took just one peek at them, but it told me enough. They don't leave my pocket again till I turn them over to Colonel Jameson down at the fort yonder. This fellow's a spy. And he's a dangerous one. We're lugging him off to Jameson on the double quick."

"You're lugging yourself into a peck of trouble!" I roared in exasperation. "General Arnold will have you all three by the heels in the guardhouse for this. You're making a blunder that will cost the cause much."

"By the looks of those papers of his," answered Van Wart, "if we let him go, we'd be making a blunder that would cost the cause a heap more."

"Anderson," said I, "I'm more sorry than I can tell you that this miserable error has occurred. There seems nothing left for us to do but to thrash this trio of idiots into submission and set you on your road."

Van Wart stepped back to the wayside thicket as I spoke, and reappeared with a long rifle. This he calmly leveled at Anderson's breast.

"Cap'n Wayne," he drawled, "I've some respect and liking for you, but you're not going to stand between me and dooty. If you make one move to 'thrash this trio of idiots,' or if you make one move to set this spy free, why, I'll pump a load of lead into his heart. My rifle bullets don't ever go astray. And they move even quicker than you do."

I paused, irresolute. The three men were determined. No threats nor arguments of mine could move them from the belief that they had caught a dangerous British spy.

I knew Van Wart to be a man of his word. He had said he would shoot Anderson if I raised a finger to rescue him. And I was certain he would do it.

It was Anderson himself who solved the problem.

"I seem fated to delays," he said pleasantly. "Wayne, may I suggest a compromise that my very worthy jailers can scarce fail to accept? I will scribble a note to General Arnold, telling him of my arrest. If you will carry the note to him with all speed, he will, of course, send instant orders for my release. I shall be delayed only a few hours at most. It is better than being shot by the rifle of my long-haired, unshaven friend yonder."

"That's fair," assented Van Wart, quite unresentful of the frank description of himself. "Send General Arnold a note, if you like, by Cap'n Wayne. If you're all right, the general will set you free quick enough. In the meantime, we'll take you to the fort and see what Colonel Jameson has to say about it."

Anderson had drawn tablets and pencil from his pocket, and was writing rapidly. Paulding openly looked over the prisoner's shoulder; then grunted disgustedly.

"H-m! He's writing in cipher!"

Anderson folded the note and handed it to me.

"Ride with all the speed your horse can make," he begged with strange earnestness. "Every minute of delay may mean worse disaster than you can comprehend. *Ride,* man! Ride like the wind! Let nothing detain you."

His intent eagerness infected me. Wheeling my horse, I thundered back along the road by which I had come.

Perhaps it would have been better for my country if a ball from Van Wart's rifle had stretched me dead as I went.

Chapter XII.
An Interrupted Meal.

ALONG the road, in the roseate early morning light, I dashed.

At about a quarter mile south of the point where I had left Edith waiting, it occurred to me that, by jumping my horse over a fence and riding across country instead of sticking to the tortuous road, I could cut off a good two miles.

Anderson had said everything depended on my haste. Surely it was more needful that Arnold should receive the cipher note without delay and send word to release Anderson upon his all-important mission to New York than that I should waste time stopping to explain matters to Edith.

At best, her lover could not now return to her. Her lamed horse, while unable to travel rapidly, could eventually carry her back to headquarters.

Sorely tempted as I was to turn aside for a word with her, I felt that military duty ordered me most imperatively to deliver the note to Arnold with all speed.

If Anderson were to reach New York on time to carry out his mysterious mission for our cause, Arnold must send post-haste to release him from the ignorant zealots into whose hands he had fallen.

I put my horse at the fence, cleared it, and was galloping across a stubble field. Somewhere westward, a bare quarter-mile away, a girl was straining her ears to catch the hoof-beats of her sweetheart's horse.

And I, who might have borne a word of comfort to her, was riding past on a call of duty. I steeled my mind to the thought and hastened on.

Past the old boat-house I rode. I noted that the Vulture had returned to her midstream mooring. I drew rein at the front door of the Beverly Robinson house, swung to the ground, leaving my tired horse standing there, and hurried up the walk.

"Has General Arnold left for his morning rounds?" I asked of the aide who was lounging on the porch.

"Not he," answered the officer. "He is inside, acting as host at a state feast. General Washington arrived from Hartford not a half-hour ago. De Lafayette and Hamilton are with him. All are eating a late breakfast. If you value the general's favor, do not intrude. They are having too merry a meal to brook interruption on pretext of dull business."

As he spoke, the sound of gay laughter came to us from the dining-room beyond. I could detect Arnold's hearty mirth above the rest.

It irked me to break in upon such a scene, yet I strode down the hall, past the sentry at the door, and on into the sunlit apartment.

Facing me as I opened the door, and at the table's head, sat George Washington. His broad face looked tired, his buff-and-blue uniform was dusty from long riding. Yet there was a pleasant, even genial, light in his stern blue eyes as he leaned forward to catch every word of a story one of the party was telling.

At his left sat a slender, distinguished-looking young fellow of distinctly foreign aspect. I had seen him but once before. He was the youthful Marquis de Lafayette, the French hero who had cast in his fortune with the Colonies.

At his excellency's right sat Madam Arnold, bewitchingly pretty and little more than a girl in years. (In fact, she was barely nineteen.)

Farther down the table was Alexander Hamilton. He it was who was telling the story which seemed to be amusing them all so much. At the foot of the board, his back to me, sat Arnold.

"Yes," Hamilton was saying, "ashore they came like a river god and a goddess of the deep, dripping wet and seemingly fished out of midstream. I asked Wayne—why, *hallo!*" he broke off on sight of me, "speaking of angels, we behold them. Here is the man in the case. And, this time, quite dry. Mayhap he will tell us the rest of the tale."

I paid no heed to this banter nor to the merry suggestions it evoked. Clicking my heels together, I drew myself up and saluted his excellency, then stepped forward to Arnold's side.

As I did so, he turned about in his chair to greet me. His eyes met mine.

And from the quick change in his face he must have seen something was amiss. Yet, in an instant, he was his jovial self again.

"Well, lad," said he familiarly, "what new duty comes to break in upon our pleasant meal? You look fagged. A glass of wine?"

"I thank you, sir," I answered formally. "I have ridden hard to bring you this."

And I handed him Anderson's note. He took it carelessly. With a word of apology to General Washington, he opened and glanced over the single sheet of cipher-scrawled paper.

I expected an outbreak of temper as he read of the miscarrying of his latest military plan. I looked to see him redden, mutter in anger, or at the very least to hear him relate ruefully to his guests how the stupidity of three militiamen had delayed an important bit of secret-service work.

Instead, not a muscle of his handsome face stirred. Nor did he change color, nor volunteer any explanation. He merely thrust the note into his pocket and rose from the table.

"I crave your excellency's pardon," he said gracefully. "I must absent myself for a moment to give an order. By the way," he added, as if in afterthought, laying his hand on my arm, "have I your excellency's permission to present and commend to your notice my aide, Captain Philip Wayne?"

I bowed low. Washington returned my salutation with a kindly smile and a word of greeting.

"Captain Wayne," pursued Arnold, "is not only the hero of Hamilton's monstrous witty story, but of many a hard-fought fight. Also he is my dear friend. I wish that your excellency at some future day might reward his services as I have not the power to do."

Embarrassed by his praise and at the somewhat surprised glances of the company, I bowed again, and prepared to follow my leader from the room.

At the threshold Arnold paused. As though moved by some sudden, uncontrollable impulse, he walked back to the table, leaned over his wife's chair, and kissed that decidedly astonished young lady on the forehead.

Then he hurried out without a word.

"Faith!" exclaimed his excellency, "General Arnold is as ardent a lover as he is a gallant soldier and patriot. I can give him no higher praise."

"If it be gallantry," put in De Lafayette with his strong French accent, "to make us all mad with envy by the exercise of such loverlike privileges, then General Arnold is a veritable paladin."

I waited to hear no more, but followed Arnold's receding figure.

He did not speak to me, but limped hurriedly down the hall and to the front door.

There, catching sight of my horse at the gate, he hastened across the walk and threw himself into the saddle.

"Good-by, dear lad!" he called to me.

I think he said more, but the clatter of his horse's hoofs drowned the words.

I stared after him. Of course I guessed his intent. He was going in person to set Anderson free.

It was ever like him to do things for himself that a hundred others could have done quite as well for him. Yet I wondered that he should excuse himself to Washington, saying he must absent himself "for a moment," and then to leave all his guests in the lurch while he started off on a twenty-mile ride. I could not understand.

But one thing I realized: The horse he had mounted was far too weary to make this new journey. He would be worn out ere the route was half traversed.

An orderly passed, leading a saddled troop charger fresh from the stables. I hailed him, jumped to the saddle, and rode off in Arnold's wake.

I knew I should soon overtake his tired mount. Then, if Arnold should still insist on making the journey, I would give him the fresh horse for the purpose.

Down the southward road I raced. As I neared the boat-house I saw the other horse standing riderless in the road. Fearful lest the general had been thrown, I galloped up, drew rein, and looked about me anxiously.

No sign of him could I see, nor did he answer my call.

At length my eyes fell upon a fast-rowed skiff that had evidently just put out from the boat-house. Its sole occupant was Benedict Arnold. He was rowing with might and main.

Stupidly I stared after him. What, in the name of all that was plausible, did this mean?

He had excused himself from the table "for a moment," had mounted a horse apparently bound on a ride to Tarrytown, and had, a half-mile farther on, abandoned the saddle and was now rowing across to West Point.

No, not to West Point, for he was shaping his course to the southward. If he should hold that direction long enough he might run straight into the anchored British war-sloop Vulture. In which case he would infallibly be captured and dragged to New York a prisoner.

I was too far away to hail him or to catch up to him in another boat. I could only stand stupefied. Nearer and nearer he approached the war-sloop.

At last—I could not believe my eyes—he reached the Vulture, parleyed a minute or two with her captain (who leaned over the rail to speak to him), and actually climbed a companion-ladder that was hastily let down over the side.

The Vulture's anchor was raised and she sped southward.

Was I insane? What did it mean?

Chapter XIII.
The Revelation.

I TURNED the incomprehensible matter over and over in my mind. Benedict Arnold was commandant of West Point. He had rowed out to a British war-sloop, and had been received on board with every mark of welcome.

It was not possible. But it was true.

Also, the vessel had carried him south toward New York, the British stronghold. He had not gone as a prisoner, but willingly—of his own initiative.

Out of the blur of impossibility a solution came to me. The ship had been more than two miles away from me. I had supposed her to be the Vulture because the Vulture had been lying somewhat farther down-stream the preceding day. Far more likely it was one of our own war-ships whose general appearance was somewhat like the Vulture's.

Yes. Of course that was the secret of the puzzle. Had not the Vulture been scared away from her moorings, north of Teller's Point, the night before?

Was it likely she would return so soon and come so much farther up the river? Naturally not.

Now, I was sure I saw the whole idea. Arnold had left the breakfast-table to write out an order for Anderson's release. Seeing my horse at the gate he had conceived the notion of riding to Tarrytown in person.

By the time he had gone half a mile he found the horse was exhausted. Noticing one of our sloops offshore, he had decided he could go to Tarrytown more quickly by water than by returning home for a fresh horse.

I could have laughed at the simplicity of the whole thing. Then, remembering suddenly that I had not slept for nearly thirty hours, and that I had not breakfasted, I mounted one of the horses and, leading the other, went back to headquarters.

Eating a hearty meal at the officers' mess, I sought my own room. There I undressed, bathed, and threw myself on the bed. I was asleep almost as soon as my head sank into the pillow.

DARKNESS had fallen when I started up with an exclamation of surprise. Some one had entered my room and was flashing a lantern into my eyes.

My blinking, sleepy gaze managed to discern that the lantern-bearer was Hamilton and that his gay young face was very grave.

"Wayne," he said, "his excellency wishes to speak to you. At once."

To be honored by a personal summons from George Washington was no light thing. I recalled Arnold's commendation of me to his excellency. Apparently, that same commendation was bearing early fruit.

Perhaps I was to be entrusted with some important command. Possibly, even, I was to be invited to join the general staff. Who could say? Hamilton's unwonted gravity bespoke something of import.

Even as I pondered, I was dressing with all the easy haste a soldier so readily learns. As I thrust my feet into my boots and stood up, ready, I reached for my sword.

"I do not think you will need that," said Hamilton, speaking for the first time since his announcement of the chief's message.

I vaguely wondered at his remark. But I paid no further heed to it and buckled the sword-belt about me as I followed him out of the barracks.

Across the lawn he led me, toward the main house. A clock was striking eight. I must have been asleep for nearly ten hours. I wondered if, by this time, Anderson had been set free; and what punishment Arnold had meted out to the silly militiamen who had detained him.

Into the house we went. At the closed door of the drawing-room Hamilton said a word to the sentinel on guard there. The man stood aside, Hamilton opened the door, motioned me to precede him into the room, followed me thither, and closed the door behind him.

In the big, low-ceiled, candle-lit apartment, a half-dozen men were grouped about a center-table littered with papers.

I recognized in a casual glance "Mad Anthony" Wayne (dressed as ever, as though for a ball), De Lafayette, General Ralph Dale, and one or two others whom I knew personally or by sight. I did not see Arnold, and concluded he had not yet returned.

Washington was at the table's head. An air of funereal hush and solemnity pervaded the whole room.

General Washington, as I halted before him and saluted, looked up at me with a stern, steady glance that seemed to pierce my very soul.

His blue eyes were as cold and hard as a frozen river. He did not return my salute.

The other men at the table were eying me with eagerness, some with a decidedly unfriendly—nay, suspicious—air. Even Mad Anthony, who bore the same name as myself and who always had a jolly word for me, did not smile as our glances met. The silence waxed oppressive.

"Your excellency sent for me?" I ventured to ask at last.

I felt strangely ill at ease. The more so as Washington did not reply at once. After an instant's pause, during which his eyes did not once leave my face, he said:

"Captain Wayne, you will give us, as briefly as possible, an exact account of your movements during the past twenty-four hours."

I stared at him in dull amaze. What was the meaning of such a question? I glanced around the circle of hard, inquiring faces.

"Your excellency," I replied, "is this a court martial? Am I on trial?"

"In a sense, yes," returned the chief. "Answer my question."

Again, as usual, I jumped to a conclusion. News of the unknown traitor, "Gustavus," and of his treasonable correspondence, had, no doubt, been reported by Arnold to Washington. An inquiry was afoot. And I—to judge by the faces about me—was somehow suspected.

A hot flush of wrath at such injustice reddened my cheeks. At sight of it, one or two men nudged each other.

"If I am on trial," I cried boldly, "I demand, as my right, to hear the charge."

"You young idiot!" roared Mad Anthony, whom the presence of even the highest authority could never awe into silence, "don't quibble like that. Answer his excellency's question and tell a straight story. Take my word, it's your best chance."

Beneath his bluff tone I seemed to detect a covert friendliness. And it impelled me to follow his advice.

"It is now eight o'clock," I began, speaking with the exaggerated formal manner of one delivering a dry report. "My movements since 8 P.M. yesterday, to the best of my memory, are as follows: I finished copying certain routine post-reports for General Arnold, then went for a walk—"

"Where and with whom?" asked Washington.

"Southward and alone," I retorted. "I walked for perhaps three miles along the East Bank road, then returned. Reaching the boathouse, a half-mile below here, I took a skiff and crossed the river; landed some distance north of King's Point; remained in that vicinity for perhaps one hour, returned to headquarters, saddled two horses, rode southward to Ferguson's Farms, then northward for one mile, then south again to North Tarrytown, then back to headquarters; then—"

"What hodgepodge is this?" growled Mad Anthony. "What d'ye mean by—"

"His excellency," I returned, "has demanded an exact and brief account of my movements for the past twenty-four hours. I am trying to make that account as brief and as exact as I can."

A murmur of disapproval at my impertinence ran through the company. But Mad Anthony grinned.

"The lad has mettle, your excellency," he commented. "I was right. He is no traitor. Or if he is, he has the brazen assurance of an—"

"Traitor?" I echoed with a shout. "Your excellency! Is *that* the charge against me? This is a matter for swords, not words. I demand to face my accuser."

Washington frowned. Yet somehow I fancied he was not ill-pleased with my answer.

"Your excellency," put in Ralph Dale, in his pleasant, low-pitched voice, "may I venture to suggest that a man whom I have known for years to be loyal and brave—and whom I still believe to be so—is being allowed to labor under a misapprehension? Perhaps if he were permitted to speak more fully he might—"

"Perhaps you are right," conceded Washington. "With treason in the very air, and the fearful knowledge that has come to us to-day, we are all apt to be over-suspicious. Captain Wayne," he went on more gently, "you crossed the river last night, you say. Why?"

"In pursuit of two boats. One was following the other. I followed the second."

"Who were the occupants of those boats?"

"Your excellency," I said in dire embarrassment, "I beg you will not insist on knowing. The matter does not—"

"Captain Wayne," Washington interrupted, "as commander-in-chief of the army, I demand, on your oath of obedience, that you answer my questions."

"In the first boat," said I, "was General Benedict Arnold. In the second—"

I paused. Oath or no oath, I would not drag Edith Bliss's name into this. To my surprise, I was saved the trouble.

"You need not mention the name of the second boat's occupant," was the chief's unexpected reply. "You followed both boats across? Well?"

"I lost sight of General Arnold," I said, grateful for the respite, "and I followed—the occupant of the second boat."

"You caught up with the occupant of this boat?"

"Yes, your excellency. In a glade about a furlong from the river."

"This—this person was alone?"

"No. A man had joined—"

"Was this man General Arnold?"

"No, sir. General Arnold arrived a few minutes later. After—after the person I had followed was gone."

"General Arnold spoke to the man who had been talking to this person?"

"Yes, your excellency. They met by appointment."

"How do you know?" snapped Mad Anthony, as the others leaned forward in sudden interest.

"General Arnold told me so. The man was an agent he was sending to New York on secret service. They met there because—"

"This agent's name? You heard it?"

"Certainly. General Arnold introduced me to him. His name is John Anderson, a Continental officer. I mistook him for the Anderson who had conducted the traitorous correspondence of which your excellency has doubtless heard. Under that misapprehension, I throttled him. General Arnold convinced me that I was mistaken, and I apologized."

Question after question brought out the other events of the night and of the morning. I told everything frankly, with the sole omission of Edith Bliss's name.

When I reached the point of my narrative where she had met me and bade me turn back to recall Anderson, I referred to her as "the occupant of the second boat," and Washington did not press me for a closer description.

I ended my tale with telling how Arnold had rowed out to a ship in midstream and had sailed southward on her.

"The name of that ship?" asked Washington.

"I do not know, your excellency. A war-sloop, built so much on the lines of the Vulture that I should have thought it was she, had not General Arnold boarded her."

"You would have been correct in your surmise," said the chief very quietly. "The sloop *was* the Vulture."

"Then how did General Arnold happen to—to—"

"He sailed on her to New York, to his new masters, the British," replied Washington with infinite sadness.

I stared agape. Surely I had misunderstood! Or else the chief had made a most ludicrous slip of the tongue.

I wondered that nobody laughed.

"Do you know who John Anderson is?" queried Washington, noting my dull astonishment.

"An officer of our army. General Arnold told me. I do not know to what regiment he belongs."

"He belongs to General Clinton's personal staff," answered Washington. "He is Major John André, of the British army. And he acted as go-between when Benedict Arnold bargained with Clinton to sell his country. Arnold fled to the Vulture to escape a traitor's punishment."

"You lie!" I yelled in blind fury, snatching out my sword. "Commander-in-chief or not, you *lie!*"

Chapter XIV.
I Learn Terrible News.

ON the instant, every man in the room was on his feet. The candle-light flashed from quick-drawn blades. A half-dozen sword-points menaced me.

I did not care. Stung to insanity of rage by this vilest of calumnies toward my adored leader, I was ready at that moment to fight the whole Continental Army, man by man, in defense of my general's loyalty.

Washington alone remained calm in the sudden turmoil. He had not moved from his seat; nor had his wise, immobile face changed its look of calm grief.

He was still eying me searchingly. Yet in his gaze I could read no rage at my act of audacity in giving him the lie and drawing weapon against him.

"Sheathe your swords!" he ordered with that quiet authority which was more irresistible than any other man's wildest eloquence. "Sheathe your swords, gentlemen, and resume your seats."

One by one the men obeyed, until I alone was standing before him with unsheathed blade and scowling face.

"Your excellency," cried Hamilton amid the babel, "you are too high to resent this blackguard's insult in person. Give me leave to challenge him and to avenge you!"

The chief's eyes turned with affectionate forbearance toward this best-loved member of his staff.

"Hamilton," he said, "if a man were to tell you I were a traitor—that I was selling my country to the enemy—what would you do?"

"Do?" echoed Hamilton. "He should not live to finish his abominable speech!"

"Can you then blame Captain Wayne for giving me the lie when I told him of Arnold's treachery? He loved Arnold. For five years he had been Arnold's chosen aide. To him Arnold represented all that was noblest in manhood. By insulting me and by drawing sword, he has not only proven his loyalty to Arnold, but—in my eyes, at least—to the cause as well."

By this time I was gasping dazedly at him. My sword-point had sunk to the floor. My head whirled as if in vertigo, and my knees shook under me.

The whole universe—my universe—had fallen about me. I was incapable of clear thought.

All I knew was that my general had just been accused of the most hideous of crimes, and that his accuser was a man whose truthfulness and justice had already passed into a proverb.

Through my whirlwind of conflicting thoughts came the chief's calm voice. He was speaking once more to me, and now in a tone a father might use toward a sorrowing child.

All at once I realized his greatness was such that my puny insolence had not so much as reached him.

"Sit down, Captain Wayne," he said, pointing to a chair near his side.

Instinctively I obeyed him, for indeed I was on point of collapsing. I sank into the chair, my head on my breast, my unsheathed sword still dangling in my nerveless fingers.

"Captain," the chief went on, "I require no apology from you for the words you just used toward me. They and your resentment clear away any last doubts of your honesty. We had already made as sure of that as possible. But your own testing was needed to banish such lingering suspicions as must be in all our hearts this night. For, when Benedict Arnold betrays, whom can we trust?"

I half started up with another furious protest on my lips. But he waved me back and continued:

"You knew Arnold well. Then you knew how dear to me he was and how implicitly I trusted him. Think you, is your grief greater than mine? I would have staked my soul on his loyalty. Now that he is false, it is as though the solid earth were cut away from before my feet."

By an effort, I tore my eyes away from a bit of colored cambric on the floor on which my gaze had been unconsciously focused, and turned to the chief.

"General Arnold has been accused?" said I. "Will your excellency not suspend judgment until he is here to answer the charge? Believe me, he will clear himself in a single word. Or may *I* not act as his representative and face down his accuser? It is not the first foul slander urged against him by his foes and by your own."

For answer, Washington took from the table a thin packet of papers. He drew one sheet from the packet and handed the rest to me.

"Examine those," said he. "Examine them carefully."

I did so. On a dozen sheets of tissue paper were traced plans, diagrams, etc., with subjoined lists of arms, men, and provisions. Stupidly I went on from page to page.

"What are those documents?" asked Washington as I came to the end.

"A full outline of our position at West Point and the Highland forts," I returned, "and complete lists of equipments."

"You are certain?"

"I ought to be," said I. "I made them out myself. See, they are in my handwriting."

"When did you do this?"

"It was a task General Arnold set me when he went on his recent tour of the Catskill forts. I copied them from his official maps and ledgers."

"To what purpose?"

"He desired this duplicate set, he said, to forward to your excellency at Hartford, which he evidently did, as you have them."

"On the contrary," replied Washington, "I saw them this night for the first time. They were forwarded to me from Tarrytown by Colonel Jameson, who is in command there. They were found hidden in the boots of 'John Anderson'—or André—when he was captured this morning. He was bearing them to Clinton."

"He stole them, then!" I cried, "and he has played General Arnold false. The general believed him a loyal man, and was sending him on secret service to New York. He told me so himself, and ordered me to ride as far with Anderson as Ferguson's Farms. If this be the sole evidence against General Arnold, I—"

Washington handed me the single paper he had abstracted from the list. I glanced it over. And in that reading I felt myself all at once become an old man.

It was a letter, signed with Arnold's name and unquestionably in the strong handwriting wherewith I was so familiar. It even contained the odd turns of speech which were so characteristic of his letters.

I shall not here repeat its contents, although their every word is still burned into my memory. I shall but briefly cite the letter's general trend.

It was addressed to General Clinton, and told of sending by Major André the accompanying full details of our Hudson strongholds. It spoke, in passing, of the long secret correspondence between himself and André when they had respectively addressed each other as "Gustavus" and "John Anderson, Merchant."

The letter went on to reiterate an arrangement whereby the British were to sail in force against West Point, which Arnold, after a faint show of resistance, should surrender to them.

It ended with an acceptance of Clinton's "generous offer of 10,000 pounds sterling and a brigadier-generalship in the British army, in payment for these services."

I know not how long I glared at this horrible, unbelievable letter, nor how often I read it and reread it. My heart seemed dead within me. Here was evidence that even I could not doubt.

At last I raised my ghastly, miserable face to the chief. In his sad eyes I read sympathy that well-nigh unnerved me. Trembling, I rose to my feet and laid my sword upon the table before him.

"Your excellency," I made shift to say, "I once thought I would be willing to follow Benedict Arnold to the world's end. I cannot follow him to my country's foes. Yet it is not meet that I who have been his friend should serve where daily I shall hear his name cursed. I beg to withdraw from the army."

"We have this day lost a traitor whom we trusted," replied Washington. "Must the cause be further weakened by the loss of a gallant, loyal officer? Reconsider, I beg of you. If *I* can endure this, then assuredly *you* can."

I read the meaning beneath his words. What capital his enemies in Congress and in the army would make of this.

How they would sneer at the chief's judgment of men, now that his dearest, most trusted friend had turned traitor!

Compared with Washington's misfortune, my own was but as a pin-scratch. I wondered at his unselfish forbearance toward me at the time.

With a bow I stretched out my hand to take back my sword, but the chief's own fingers fell upon the blade and held it there. I looked at him in astonishment.

"Wait," he said formally.

Then, to the others, he resumed:

"Captain Philip Wayne of General Arnold's staff has voluntarily laid down his commission, and he cannot take it up again at will."

He paused a moment. Remorse shot through me like a knife. Of old I had grumbled at my thankless service in a hopeless cause. Yet now, in a flash, I saw how precious that service and that cause were to me.

And I grieved unspeakably at my self-enforced banishment from them. Yet I muttered:

"It's but just. I bow to your excellency's decree."

"It *is* but just," he assented, with the same formality, "that Captain Philip Wayne of General Arnold's staff should not resume his commission. But"—proffering me my own sword—"I beg to restore this weapon to *Major* Philip Wayne, of General Washington's personal staff. Gentlemen, the session is at an end."

Chapter XV.
Edith to the Rescue!

I stood alone on the lawn in the darkness. My head was still awhirl, my heart like lead.

I was at last on the road to high promotion. I was a major on Washington's staff, to serve under his own eye.

It was such a chance as I had craved for years. Yet, for the moment, it was as Dead Sea fruit to my palate, in face of the tragedy that encompassed me.

I could not yet recover sufficiently from the numbness of the shock to think clearly.

Across the lawn toward me came Ralph Dale.

"I want to congratulate you on your appointment, Wayne," said he, "and to tell you how sorry all of us are for the loss that's come to you. Would you care to hear the details? If not, say so. But, since you *must* hear them soon or late, I thought they would come less cruelly from the lips of a friend."

I nodded. In his modulated, expressive voice, the ex-actor told me the story of my leader's shame, as the later developments of the day had brought it to light.

Here, in as few words as I can, I will set down the gist of what he said. It is a story all Americans should know, even though it is the bitter narrative of a valiant man's degradation—a hero's fall to perdition.

For years Arnold had suffered persecution. He had borne it bravely until the final disgrace of the Philadelphia court martial. Then a veritable devil of revenge began to possess him.

Placed in charge of our strongest, all-important fortress, he plotted to sell it and the whole cause to our enemies.

He had opened correspondence with Clinton, who used Major André, his adjutant, as intermediary. After long correspondence, André had sailed up the Hudson in the Vulture to meet Arnold in person at a spot outside the lines, there to make the final arrangements and to receive the promised plans of West Point.

While they were conferring, the cannon-shots from Teller's Point had scared the Vulture away. André had been in a quandary.

Up to that point he had merely been an emissary and had acted well within the rules of warfare.

Now, however, he was forced to enter the enemy's lines in order to get back to New York. He could not do this in uniform. To do so in civilian clothes would make him a spy.

Yet there was no alternative. Going to the house of a Tory, he had procured a riding-suit and, armed with Arnold's pass and my escort, had traveled safely enough until, twenty-seven miles from New York, Van Wart and the two other militiamen had seized him.

Then, realizing the hopelessness of his own plight, and knowing that the papers he carried would condemn both Arnold and himself, he had bravely sought to save his accomplice.

The cipher note I had carried to Arnold was a warning from André that all was lost. The general had read it, excused himself to his guests, mounted my horse, ridden to the boat-house, and had thence rowed out to the Vulture, which had returned up-stream at daylight in search of André.

"I would give my right hand to get André out of this," finished Dale. "He saved my life once. I've interceded for him with the chief. But it is no use. Washington is adamant. The man must hang—Heaven help him! He has been taken to Tappan. We start thither at midnight. By the way, Phil, things looked black for you at one time."

"When I drew sword on the chief?" I asked.

"No. An hour earlier. There can be no harm in telling you now. We had news that it was you who escorted André through the lines, that you tried to free him from his captors, that you had brought the warning to Arnold, that the plans and other papers found on André were in your handwriting. The chief was about to order your arrest when—"

"I scarce blame him," I interrupted. "A less great commander would have hanged a man on far slighter evidence. What deterred him?"

"Miss Edith Bliss."

"I—I do not understand."

"She demanded audience with the chief. And a strange enough story she told. She spoke first of a letter she had shown you a week or so ago—a letter from Gustavus to André. She said you refused to speak to her afterward about it and—"

"I had promised Arnold."

"She did not know that. It roused her suspicion. She saw a cloaked man cross the Hudson last night. Thinking it was you, and that you were on a treasonable errand, she followed."

"And *I* followed *her*," I put in.

"So it seems. She met André there. You came up, while she slipped into the shadows of the woods, and she speedily heard enough to convince her of your innocence. But she suspected Arnold. She could not imagine why he should be meeting André there secretly. When the two went away alone to talk, leaving you on guard, she followed them."

I recalled the vague shape I had seen slipping across the moonlit glade.

"She heard enough to tell her the whole story," went on Dale. "She followed when André and Arnold recrossed the river. But she found her skiff had floated away. She had to tramp for miles along the west bank before she could find another. It was almost dawn when she reached headquarters. She found you had ridden on with André. She dared not tell any one. So she followed, hoping to get back the papers."

Oh, the gallant, *gallant* girl! Then it had not been merely to bid André farewell that she had galloped so furiously.

"She told the chief her story," added Dale. "It almost wholly cleared you. Your own outrageous conduct killed whatever remaining suspicion may have lingered in our minds. I congratulate you on such a lovely advocate."

"Her sorrow to-night is even greater than ours," I answered simply. "She loves André."

"No?"

"She loves him. Last night, when she thought I was about to fight him, she besought me with tears and wild entreaties to spare him. And," I went on, "if he and she had not loved each other, would she have so relied on her power over him, when she found what he really was, as to ride after him this morning for the purpose of persuading him to give her the papers he carried? Poor child! It is a black hour for her."

Dale eyed me strangely.

"Phil," he said at last, "you are a good soldier. But you are more of a dunce. I won't explain. You wouldn't understand. Come! The bugle is sounding. We start for Tappan at once. A new chapter in history in beginning this day."

Chapter XVI.
The Raid.

A RAMBLING story-and-a-half farmhouse, with Dutch doors and two circular windows. In front, a dusty road. Behind, a forest whose leaves were turning to autumn tints. This was General Washington's headquarters at Tappan.

Ralph Dale and I came out of the house and started, side by side, down the road. Our faces were sober. This was the day set for John André's execution. We had gone together to make a final appeal to the chief for clemency. And, we had been refused.

Now we were on our way to the guardhouse where André was lodged. For we were to accompany him to the scaffold.

It had taken but few days to try and condemn André. He had denied nothing, and had merely asked that he be shot as a soldier, not hanged as a spy.

The British government had deigned to intercede most vehemently for him. But to all pleas Washington was deaf. The fate of the Colonies had been at stake.

Arnold, safe in New York, could not be punished. But an example to traitors must be made. And André alone remained.

It had been a busy, sad time for me. I liked the gay young fellow who must meet so terrible a fate. I was doubly miserable at thought of Edith Bliss's sorrow.

I had not seen nor heard of the girl since that tragic day at Arnold's hedquarters. Nor, try as I would, could I gain news about her. Now that the Arnold household was disrupted, I knew not what had become of her.

I pictured her as penniless, out of employment, alone, weighted down with the grief of her lover's impending death. And I would have given my life to be of use to her in her time of sorrow and destitution.

More than once I was conscious of a horribly unworthy thought. In later days, might not her mourning for André be so softened as to permit me to urge my own love upon her? But I put the tempting reflection from me with shame at my own baseness.

To-day, as Dale and I trudged silently side by side toward the guard-house, Mad Anthony Wayne emerged from his hut, fastening on his sword, and joined us.

"This is sorry business!" he growled. "You remember André's 'Cow Chase' song, and how it ended by expressing a fear *lest that same warrior-drover Wayne should ever catch the poet'*? Well, by a twist of Fate, *I'm* detailed to superintend the execution. The poor lad!"

A man, coatless, disheveled, passed along the road ahead of us, half led, half dragged by six infantrymen.

"A deserter," observed Wayne. "Some of my Riders caught him making for New York, and brought him in. He is being taken to the outer guard-house, just beyond the scaffold."

The deserter and his guard had just reached a little belt of woodland that lined the road. They were scarce a hundred yards ahead of us.

As Mad Anthony finished speaking, a quick volley of rifle-shots spurted from the undergrowth of the woods.

Two of the deserter's guards pitched over headlong. A third staggered back, nursing a bullet-riddled arm.

Out of the woods swooped a dozen mounted men, dressed as

trappers. In a rush they rode down the three other guards.

Then they snatched up the utterly bewildered deserter and hoisted him to the back of a led horse.

The whole maneuver had not occupied five seconds. We three officers stood, dumfounded, watching it.

One of the mounted trappers—a broad-shouldered, heavily bearded negro—leaned forward and scanned the deserter's face. Then, in an angry, chagrined voice, he shouted something to his comrades.

One of them, with a blow of his fist, knocked the deserter from the saddle. Leaving the fallen man sprawling in the road, the whole party galloped off at breakneck speed.

Dale clapped a hand to his pistol.

"No use!" said Mad Anthony. "They are out of range. In another half minute they'll be out of sight."

Soldiers, drawn by the noise of firing, came rushing up from all directions. The deserter had got to his feet, wriggled into a thicket and escaped.

While the wounded guards were lifted and carried away, Dale stood mute. Then, of a sudden, he burst out, cutting in on Mad Anthony's flood of profane conjecture. "I have it!" he cried. "Those men are no trappers. They have the military seat in the saddle. The *British* military seat at that. They are soldiers. British soldiers. It was a rescue-party that had smuggled its way through the lines and—"

"To rescue a Yankee deserter from the guard-house?" scoffed Wayne.

"No," replied Dale. "To rescue John André from the gallows."

"*What?*"

"Exactly that. They knew where the scaffold stands. They supposed André was to be brought thither direct from headquarters (as was planned yesterday, before the order came to lodge him for the night in the outer guard-house). They lay in wait. When they saw a prisoner dragged along this road in the direction of the scaffold, they supposed it was André. That bearded negro was the first to see their mistake. So they unhorsed the deserter and rode on. A daring trick!"

"But," sputtered Mad Anthony, only half convinced, "if they were British troops, why were they led by that negro? I never heard of any negro in the British army. Least of all, in command."

"Yon was no negro," retorted Dale. "Far away from us as he was, I could see that. I was not an actor for ten years without knowing something of disguise. The man's face was blacked. His features were half hidden behind that great, bushy beard. But those that were visible were not negro features. No, and I'll wager the beard was false as well."

"A brave scoundrel, whoever he was!" declared Mad Anthony. "For, by that raid, he was leading his men into the lion's very jaws. If they were British soldiers, they were within the American lines in civilian garb. And that means death by hanging, as even poor André knows. Every rider in that band risked the rope in his dash to save the fellow."

He called up an orderly and gave a brief command.

"To prevent our trapper friends from coming back for another attempt," he said as we moved on, "I've ordered a hundred men to patrol the woods and two hundred more to guard the scaffold. I should like another glimpse at that bearded negro," he added, half to himself. "Something about his figure or the way he rode was oddly familiar. Perhaps I have seen him in battle or at a flag-of-truce conference."

We reached the guard-house. Even the rough sentries at the door looked gloomy.

André had endeared himself to every one with whom he had come in contact. The first resentment past, the American public had learned to regard him not as a monster of crime, but as a brave soldier caught while doing his simple, perilous duty to his king and his commander.

All pitied him. Even Washington, had expediency permitted, would, I think, have welcomed a chance to pardon him.

As we halted before the guard-house door, André came forth, one of Mad Anthony's "Riders" on either side of him. A provost-marshal's man, cords in hand, drew near.

"Gentlemen," said André, smiling as he caught sight of us, "I bid you good morning. I take it gratefully that you are to honor me with your company to this swiftest and longest of my many journeys."

"André," growled bluff old Anthony Wayne, "I'd give a thousand pounds—which I don't possess—and ten years of my life if I could get you free of this. You are a brave man. Too brave and too good to have been mixed up with that accursed blackguard Arnold."

"I thank you," bowed André.

Then, in a flash of his old infectious gaiety, he said:

"It seems I was a prophet. The 'warrior-drover, Wayne,' has at last 'caught the poet.' And—"

He broke off. The provost-marshal's deputy had laid hold of his wrists to bind them with the cords.

"Is this necessary?" André asked of Mad Anthony.

And I think the pain and the appeal in his eyes struck every one of us to the heart.

"'Tis customary," muttered Wayne; "but—custom or no custom, you sha'n't be degraded like this. The chief can berate me afterward, if he will, for neglect of duty. Deputy, throw those filthy cords away! Major André, will you give me your word of honor to make no effort at escape on your way to the—to—to your destination?"

"Willingly," assented the prisoner.

"Then you shall walk with us unbound, and as a gentleman among gentlemen," declared Mad Anthony. "Forward all!"

"Major," I said to André in a low voice, as our sad little procession moved down the road, "I shall seek to find Mistress Bliss as soon as I can get a few days free from duty. Can I bear her any message, or last token from you? If so, command me."

He flushed with surprise, and his lips parted to reply. But at that moment we came to a turn in the road.

Before us, a hundred yards distant, rose the scaffold. Around its foot were ranged a double company of infantrymen.

Just beyond the line of soldiers, and pressing as close as they could to the scaffold, were a great throng of country folk from the surrounding districts.

This gaping crowd filled the whole space between the troops and the forest beyond.

At sight of the gibbet, André halted. His face went ashen gray; then a red tide of shame darkened it.

"Gentlemen," he protested, his rich voice trembling with horror, "I had not expected this! I begged his excellency that I might be shot, not hanged like a felon."

There was an awkward silence in the little group of officers. Not one of us could find a word to say.

To this hour I cannot see why justice would not have been quite as amply fulfilled had the gallant Englishman been permitted to die a soldier's death. But André saved us the trouble of answering. As quickly as fear had smitten him, so quickly did his valiant spirit shake it off.

He squared his shoulders. The old magnetic smile crept back to his white lips.

"So be it," he said calmly. "I call you all to witness that I die as a brave man should."

He moved forward again, leading us all.

From the forest, at this juncture, emerged an oddly clad figure, mounted on a magnificent bay horse. Pushing his steed recklessly through the close-packed crowd, he gained the open space before the scaffold and dashed up to us.

Above his head, with one hand, he waved a white handkerchief. But it was less this sign of truce that drew our eyes than the man's amazing costume.

He wore the gold-laced dress uniform coat of a British cavalry colonel. On his head was a plumed military hat.

But beneath the gorgeous coat was the fringed shirt of a trapper. His legs were encased in a trapper's buckskin breeches and beaded gaiters. His feet were moccasined.

The rider—a young, slenderly built man of almost effeminate type—halted in front of us. Recognizing Mad Anthony as our leader, he saluted and handed him a paper.

It was a passport signed by General Washington, admitting the bearer—"Colonel Fitzhugh Pigot, of the British army of New York, and bearer of a despatch from General Clinton"—through our lines for the space of twenty-four hours.

I remembered the colonel as having brought to the chief, on the previous evening, the last of many protests from Clinton against Major André's execution.

But at that time Pigot had been dressed from head to foot as befitted an officer of King George's army. Where he had acquired his present costume I could not guess.

"General Wayne," said Pigot in the nasal, high-pitched voice affected by British officers of that day, "as one of Major André's oldest and closest friends, I crave leave to speak to him a word of farewell. It is little to ask of your courtesy. Have I permission?"

Wayne was glowering at him in angry wonder.

"This passport," growled he, "describes a British cavalry colonel. Not a man who is soldier from the waist up and a trapper from the waist down!"

Pigot laughed. There was no trace of embarrassment in his nasal voice as he coolly replied:

"By army regulations, as you well know, the term 'uniform' applies specifically to coat and *chapeau.* And, thus far, I am appareled according to regulations. For the rest—I had the ill luck to fall into the Tap pan Zee while returning to my cutter this morning. My clothes were drenched. So I borrowed the only ones I could find. By good fortune, I was coatless when I got my ducking."

"It seems a pity," observed Anthony dryly, "that since you had to have a ducking, it could not have been in the Well of Truth. I compliment you on saving your coat and hat. Otherwise we might be reluctantly forced to hang you; as we would fain hang a certain band of mock trappers who raided our lines this morning. Oddly enough, one of them rode a horse much like your own."

"Strange coincidence!" acquiesced Pigot indifferently. "I passed such a band of mounted trappers on my way here. They were galloping as if for dear life. I asked the cause of their haste. One of them shouted, in passing, that they feared if they tarried they might have the mischance to be enrolled among Wayne's Riders."

Mad Anthony fairly purpled with wrath at this bit of cool insolence. Ralph Dale intervened.

"As I understand it, general," said he, "this harlequin-clad and somewhat loud-voiced nondescript, desires to say a word of good-by to André. If it be André's wish, may I add my petition to his? Personally, my own chief comfort in quitting the world would be the privilege of bidding an eternal farewell to persons of Colonel Pigot's sort."

Dale's speech cleared Mad Anthony's anger, as Ralph had foreseen, and made him grant a grudging assent to the Englishman's request.

Pigot dismounted and, leading his horse by the bridle, approached André, who, interested and puzzled, had remained a few paces away from us during the brief colloquy.

As all of us save Pigot had spoken in low-pitched tones, André could not have heard our rather unflattering comments on his friend.

Pigot walked up to André and grasped his hand. Then, speaking in a quick, tense whisper, he exclaimed:

"Take my horse! Mount, man, and *ride!* There is a chance."

Now, had André chosen to obey the hurried order, there is strong reason to believe he might have made a clean escape.

He was full twenty feet away from the nearest of us. Not another man of us was mounted. The woods were less than ninety yards distant.

The soldiers on guard were expecting no such move. The band of "trappers" were doubtless lurking not far off, to bear him aid.

As for Pigot, at worst, he would have been detained as prisoner of war. Military regulations would have spared his actual life.

Oh, it was a daring scheme, and a pretty one! And it was well planned and easy of achievement.

André, however, made no move to carry it out. He smiled at Pigot, whose hand he still grasped.

"*Mount,* André!" screamed Pigot as we ran excitedly toward them. "*Mount!*"

"I am under parole," said André quietly.

"Parole to a parcel of Yankee boobies!" sneered Pigot. "*Ride,* man!"

He pushed André to the horse's side. The prisoner gently disengaged himself.

"I am under parole," he repeated; "yet I thank you with all my heart."

Mad Anthony was first of us to reach the pair. He made a leap for Pigot, and seized him by the collar.

Pigot wriggled out of his coat like an eel, leaped to his horse's back, and thundered away to the woods.

"Fire!" bawled General Wayne to the soldiers.

But it was too late.

Chapter XVII.
A Strange Meeting.

IT was over.

Slipping away from the rest—we were none of us in mood for companionship—I made my way through the woods alone.

My heart was heavy at the tragedy I had just witnessed. I wanted to be by myself, to collect my shaken nerve, to throw off the sadness that gripped me.

How far and how long I wandered aimlessly through the autumn forests I do not know. But the sun was nigh to sinking as I came out upon a bit of rocky headland above the Hudson.

Tired, gloomy, I threw myself down in a mossy hollow at the summit of the rock. Below me lay the river, roseate with the sunset.

A path wound down the steep incline at my feet, leading to the tiny patch of beach at the base of the rock. At the shore was a shallop with two men at the oars. A half mile out in the Tappan Zee rode a large cutter.

All was peaceful, silent, beautiful. The quiet and loveliness of the scene calmed me. Once or twice a farmer's cart rattled along the clifftop road a few yards from where I lay. Otherwise I was undisturbed in my melancholy solitude.

Lounging idly, with half-shut eyes, I became aware of plodding, heavy steps crossing the roadway from the woods beyond. I did not raise my head until a man (coming over my rock to gain the path that led down to the distant water edge) brushed almost against my out-sprawled feet in passing.

Still, I did not look up at once. The man's legs, from knee down—the only part of him that came within my vision—were clad in moccasined buckskins such as hunters or fisherfolk used to wear.

I supposed him a fisherman on his way to his boat below, and was not interested enough to glance at him.

But as he moved to one side to avoid stepping on me, he evidently caught sight of my half-averted face. He stopped dead short and involuntarily spoke my name.

"Phil Wayne!"

At sound of that voice I was on my feet in a second, as though stung by a hornet. Before me stood a broad, rough-clad man. He was dressed as a trapper, save that a saber and a pistol hung from his cowhide belt.

His grizzled hair, uncrowned by a hat, hung about his shoulders and almost into his eyes. A monstrous beard hid his lower features. His face was the hue of a negro's.

He was, in fact, the negro trapper who had led that morning's unsuccessful raid in André's behalf. I saw that much at one glance.

Yes, and I saw more. For, at close quarters, the light of the sinking sun falling full in his eyes, I recognized the half-hidden face and uncouth figure.

The man was Benedict Arnold!

I spoke no word, but stared aghast, as at a wraith. It could not be. And yet it was.

From behind that mask of swarthiness and the tangle of false hair and beard, my old leader's compelling dark eyes were gazing across at me with a wistful eagerness that almost unmanned me.

"Phil!" he said again.

And there was a world of entreaty in his deep voice. He held out his hand. To save my soul I could not have grasped it.

He saw my repulsion, and his arm dropped listlessly back to his side.

"If it be so with *you,* lad," he murmured, "what would it be with Washington, Putnam and Dale and the rest? You were my chum, my truest, most devoted friend. You looked on me ever with a hero-worship. Yet now you will not so much as take my hand. Aye, and you glare on me as though I were a leper."

Still, I could voice no reply. It hurt me horribly to treat thus my adored old commander. Yet I could control neither body nor voice. I could only stare at him in wondering horror.

"Lad," went on Arnold, with a ghost of the winning familiarity that had always charmed me so, "you are very dear to me. Why do you shrink back from the meeting? Am I not fit to speak to? Faith, if my own aide treats me like this, what would the rest of the Continental army do, if they chanced to catch me?"

"They would cut off your left leg that was wounded at Saratoga," I returned, finding my voice at last, "and they would bury it with military honors. The rest of you they would—*hang!*"

The words spoke themselves, with no conscious volition of mine. In later years I have seen them quoted broadcast.

Arnold winced, then broke into a little laugh.

"You do not mince matters, at least," quoth he. "You regard me as a traitor. Is it not so? Yes, your eyes speak it. Yet 'tis but fair you should hear my side. Unless," he sneered, "having made up your mind to my guilt you do not wish your opinions unsettled, by any pleas for the defense."

"If there is any argument on earth," I cried impulsively, "that will give me back my shattered faith in you and will lift you to the lofty pedestal in my regard from which you hurled yourself—in Heaven's name, let me hear it!"

"Spoken like my brave, honest lad!" he exclaimed. "Have you ever heard of General Monk?"

"Monk?" I repeated. "Why, yes. Was he not the leader of the Parliamentary troops after Oliver Cromwell's death? And did he not use his military and political power to place Charles II on the throne of England?"

"That was the man," assented Arnold. "The Parliamentary party and the Protectorate were in a hopeless state. He saved the land from further anarchy and bloodshed by throwing his own great power in behalf of the Restoration. He made Charles II king and restored the old monarchy. England and all posterity look on General Monk as a hero. He *was* a hero."

"I fail to see what—"

"What his case has to do with mine? Everything! The cases are exact in parallels. The Thirteen Colonies rebelled against England. We hoped for quick freedom. Instead, five years of steady warfare have proven that our cause is hopeless. Both England and America are throwing away money and lives in a useless struggle that can have but one end—the final, crushing defeat of the Colonies."

He paused, then continued:

"By one act I sought to bring about that inevitable result more quickly, and to end the vain conflict without further shedding of my countrymen's blood. England stood ready to give us easy terms of surrender and better future treatment than was ours in the old days. A few years hence the Colonies would have blessed my name for putting an end to the barbarous war, and for giving them peace and plenty."

"You believe that?" I exclaimed. "You honestly *believe* it?"

"Believe it? I *know* it. I should have been praised by posterity as the General Monk of America. As it is, I have failed. Failed as ever I have failed—through Fate's mistreatment, not from fault of mine. Yet the result will be the same. England will win. Future ages will see my conduct in its true light and will—"

"And will brand you as a traitor—through all eternity," I answered. "You yourself know it is true. I, who looked on you as the noblest of men, cannot even bring myself to shake your hand. Nor could John André, whose soul was the soul of a knight of old. Is it thus that *honest* men are treated?"

"I have done evil that good might come!" he muttered. "If for the present I am blamed, I can bear it, knowing posterity will vindicate me."

"'Evil that good may come'?" I retorted. "Is it nothing to you that Washington's great heart is crushed by your falseness, that you have ruined *my* ideal of manhood; that gallant John André lies dead through your sin?"

"*Don't,* lad!" he begged. "'Tis not like you to speak thus! Since when have you turned judge for—"

"Since Benedict Arnold turned hypocrite," I answered.

His hand flew instinctively to his sword-hilt. I ignored his gesture and resumed:

"Yes. *Hypocrite!* You seek to justify what you know *cannot* be justified. You scrape up patriotic motives to excuse your deed, when at heart you know you betrayed your country through base personal vengeance for the way Congress has treated you. And now, you cannot be honest even in your dishonesty. How are the mighty fallen!"

At my retort—which bitterness of heart rendered far more stinging, I fear, than its mere words would imply—Arnold of a sudden flashed out into one of the sudden homicidal rages I had learned to know so well.

"Zounds!" he flared, whipping out his saber. "No Yankee whippersnapper is going to speak to me like that and live to tell it! I had it on my tongue's end to offer to take you back with me to New York and give you a commission in the British army. But the man who dare call me 'hypocrite'—"

"If the taunt rankles, 'tis because it is merited," I answered. "You offer to take me back to New York? You yourself are not yet safe back among the new friends to whom you sought to sell us."

On the word he leaped at me, weapon raised. I had bare time to spring backward to the very edge of the cliff and to draw my own sword ere his blade whizzed with lightning speed through the air where my head had just been.

I would have avoided the conflict if I could. But my heels were at the cliff edge, preventing my farther retreat. Nor could I lower my sword-point or expostulate with him, for he was attacking me with the swift, relentless fury of a wild beast.

All my strength and swordsmanly skill were needed to hold my ground on that precipitous verge. For with every atom of his force and fury he was hurling a series of incredibly swift lunges at me.

Bracing myself as best I might, I threw every sinew and faculty into repelling that ferocious assault. Our blades played like heat lightning in the sunset air.

Arnold's face, distorted by blind madness of wrath, glared into mine with a deathless hate. His blade sought my very life.

And this was the man I had loved and revered as a father! The leader who had treated me like a favored son!

Even in that moment of life-and-death struggle, I recalled Master Congreve's famed old line:

Heaven knows no rage like love to hatred turned!

I was half-score years the younger man of the two. I was taller and stronger and, I think, the better swordsman. Yet the fight was far less unequal than one might have expected.

For Arnold was battling with all the fury of his warped, violent nature, and was mad with the desire to slay me. I, on the other hand, fought with a heavy heart, and wholly on the defensive.

Not once could I forget that this opponent of mine was my former chief, the man whom I had honored above all others. It seemed to me horribly cruel and unnatural that we should thus be at each other's throats.

Twice Arnold's fierce thrusts passed my guard. Once his sword-point glanced off my belt buckle. A second time it scratched my shoulder.

I caught one smashing blow on my uplifted blade, and took advantage of the momentary parry to run in and shift my ground to some less precarious footing.

The maneuver reversed our positions. Now it was he who stood with his back to the cliff, while I was on firmer ground.

He saw what I had done, and with the bellow of an enraged bull he re-engaged me. By sheer impetus, he gradually forced the fight in such a way as to compel me to circle in order to avoid a stab.

When I was once more with my back to the edge he lunged forward again and again, throwing his full weight into each thrust, and heedless of any return blow I might strike.

And now I saw his intent. Realizing that I was the better fencer, and that he could not hope to send his blade through me, he was seeking to make me give way before him until he should be able to drive me backward over the edge of the steep shelf of rock and send me reeling into the abyss below.

The knowledge of his savage purpose made me sick. Not only at thought of my own dire peril, but that so noble a soul as Benedict Arnold's could sink to so despicable a trick.

I was in an odd position. By this time I knew full well I was his master, and that I could end the fight at any minute by brushing aside the wearied man's guard and wounding him.

Yet I could not bring myself to do it. I still fought on the defensive, refusing to take advantage of any of the dozen openings that his unstable guard presented.

Yet the unnatural combat must be brought to a close. I watched my chance. He feinted, then slashed with all his power at my head.

I guarded the blow, ran my blade down his with a peculiar sharp twist, and wrenched with terrific force.

The saber fell from his weakened hand. His body, overbalanced by the impetus of his own blow, sprawled helpless at my feet. I was obliged to draw back my own blade swiftly to keep him from falling on it.

There he tumbled, and I stood panting above him. The furious, brief duel was over.

"Strike!" he snarled up at me, foaming at the mouth in his impotent rage. "Strike, and end my life's sorry farce!"

I dropped my sword, and stretched out my hand to help him rise. As I leaned over, two huge hairy hands reached up from the cliff path behind, gripped my ankles, and jerked my feet sharply from under me.

I fell to the earth with a crash. My head struck against a bit of upcropping rock amid the moss. There was a crack that seemed like to burst my skull. And the sunset turned into a thousand dancing colors that shot all over the horizon.

I heard a loud voice saying something in Cockney English accent. I heard a reply, in Arnold's tones. Yet, so far had my senses been scattered by the knock on the head that I could catch no words that were spoken.

I tried to struggle to my feet. But at my first move some one—or something—struck me down.

And I lay writhing there, panting and fighting for consciousness; dimly wondering what my old leader would do now that I was at his mercy.

Chapter XVIII.
The End of the Trail.

MINE was ever a thick head—in more senses than one. And a mere impact with a moss-covered rock could not reduce me to that state of utter senselessness which I am told is so pleasant.

Nevertheless, for a minute or more I must have lain there, dazed, bewildered, with no clear idea of what was going on about me.

Then Arnold began bathing my hot forehead with cool water, stroking back my tumbled hair with infinite gentleness, and with so magnetically soothing a touch that I was fain to lie still, with happily shut eyes, enjoying the odd sensation.

I found, too, that he had lifted my head into his lap—an odd attention from a soldier—and that he was murmuring something to me in a curiously sweet voice. As my mind grew more settled, this phenomenon struck me vaguely as peculiar. It was unusual for a man at one moment to be thirsting for another's blood, and at the next to be seeking to heal him with such wondrous gentle solicitude.

I opened my tired eyes. And saw—not Arnold, but Edith Bliss!

Yes. She had dropped from the skies, and had changed identity with Benedict Arnold. It seemed to me then quite natural that she should, and infinitely pleasant.

Or—were she and I still in midstream where our collision with the buoy-chain had thrown us? And was the story of the past few weeks just a queer, hideous dream? That, too, seemed extremely natural. So did everything.

It was good to be so near Edith. There was something I wanted to say to her. Something I had meant to say for a long time. What was it?

Oh, yes! I wanted to tell her I loved her. Loved her—No, I had no right to say that. She loved John André. She had begged me with tears to spare his life. She had ridden after him to—

No. André was dead. I was sure I had heard so. And, if he was dead, then—

Of a sudden, recollection and sanity came back to me. I staggered to my knees and looked stupidly about me.

The sun had well-nigh sunk. Arnold was nowhere near. A shallop rowed by two men was putting off from the patch of beach far below me. In the stern sat a man in trapper's dress.

And even at that distance I recognized him as Benedict Arnold. Two British sailors were rowing him out to the vessel which would carry him safe back to New York after his unsuccessful effort to save André's life—and to take mine.

André—

I turned again to Edith. Her face was white, and her big pansy eyes alight with anxious sympathy.

"You are better?" she asked. "You are not seriously hurt?"

"I am all right," I answered somewhat unsteadily. "It—it is good, past words, to see you. You come to me like an angel of pity. I feared I might never be able to find you again."

"I came too late to help you," she replied, "though I hurried fast. I came over the rise of the hill and saw you at swords' points with a roughly dressed negro. Even as I looked, you disarmed him and he fell. Then a man dressed as a British sailor, who had been running up the cliff path from that boat, reached out and threw you."

So! That accounted for the hairy hands that had gripped me from nowhere.

I understood now. The sailors, from their boat where they had been awaiting Arnold, had seen us fighting on the cliff top, and one of them had run to the general's aid.

"The sailor drew a knife," went on Edith, "and I am sure I think he meant to stab you. But the other man interfered. Then they saw me coming and ran down the path. The other man limped. Did you wound him?"

"No," said I. "He is lame. The 'other man' was Benedict Arnold."

"*No!*"

I told her in a mere handful of words about my strange meeting with Arnold and our fight.

But it was not of Arnold I wished to talk, nor of anything on earth except her wonderful self.

"You say you 'came over the hill,'" said I. "From where? I had not known you were near us. I have made many inquiries and could learn nothing about you, try as I would."

"Did you ask General Dale?" she queried demurely.

"Dale? No. Why should I?"

"Only because I am staying with his wife," returned Edith. "I arrived last evening from my father's farm, where I have been settling the estate. Mine. Dale had asked me to spend some weeks with her here. Their house, you know, is just below the rise of the hill over there. I was walking along the cliff road—"

"And Dale never told me!" interrupting her.

"Perhaps," she suggested, "he did not think it would interest you. The famous Major Philip Wayne could scarce be expected," she went on in sad raillery, "to be interested in the affairs of a mere governess. And—"

"Ah, *don't!*" I begged. "How can you speak so? You must know—"

"And yet," she interrupted, "I seem to have heard some such words—"

"Need you remind me?" I cried miserably. "Do you suppose that I have ever forgotten for a moment my abominable rudeness? Do you think I have not bitterly cursed my own idiocy a hundred times? Aye, a thousand times! You, the most glorious woman I ever met, deigned to stoop to my level. And I—like the blind fool I was—turned my back on the wondrous friendship that I now know meant more than life to me. Small wonder you despise me!"

"But I *don't!*" she contradicted in that direct, childlike way that had once so puzzled and fascinated me. "And I, too, was to blame. I have a confession to make, Major Wayne. Will you hear it?"

My eyes must have answered for me. For she went on, hesitatingly, in that low, sweet voice of hers:

"I liked you so much. I thought you and I were going to be such good friends. When I found that Gustavus letter and brought it to you, it seemed a new bond between us. But when I spoke to you about it next day, you evaded the subject and seemed so terribly ill at ease—"

"I had promised Arnold to speak no word of it to any one," I broke in.

"I did not know that. I remembered what you had once said about being half tempted to go over to the enemy. And—I was afraid you had been tempted above your strength."

"That I was a traitor?"

"Forgive me! I didn't *want* to think it. And even then I couldn't despise you as I felt I ought to. But when I saw General Arnold cross the Hudson that night—and thought it was you—and followed—and—"

"And *I* followed *you*—" I put in.

"Oh, what must you have thought of my wild pleas to you, when you said you had 'urgent personal business' with Major André?"

"I thought—why—didn't you know I meant to fight him? Weren't you pleading with me not to?"

"*I?* I thought you were going to confer with him on some treason plan—he was in British uniform, you know—and I wanted to save you from the treachery I feared you had planned. That is my confession. Can you ever forgive me for suspecting you so unjustly?"

I scarce heard her. My dull brain was slowly gaining a gleam of intelligence.

"Next morning," I gasped, half enlightened, "when you rode after him to get back those plans of West Point? Why did you wear a pistol in your belt? To protect you from footpads?"

"Footpads? No. To demand those papers, if need arose, at pistol-point."

"You would have—have *shot* him?"

"To save my country from betrayal? Yes. A thousand times, *yes!*"

"You could not have done it," I denied, "you *could* not!"

It amazed me to hear this gentle girl speak thus fiercely. And on the very day of André's death. Now, too, for the first time I noted her face bore no signs of tears for the dead Englishman. Also it began to occur to me that she did not speak nor bear herself like a woman in sorrow. I grew puzzled once more.

"It would have been a fearful thing," she shuddered, "to take a human life! But better than that our land should fall back into English slavery. That was why I carried the pistol."

"But," I stammered aghast, "the man you loved?"

"Loved?"

"Were you not betrothed to Major John André?"

"*I?* Are you joking? You *could* not joke about a poor soldier who has just died."

"Edith," I cried, bending over her, trembling with a wild new ecstasy of excitement. "Edith! I love you! *I love you!*"

Dusk was falling as we strolled back, toward the Dale quarters.

"Dale asked me to-day if I would dine with him this evening," I said. "The scoundrel! I believe he knew everything. All along."

"I—I believe he did," shyly admitted Edith. "I thought you might come by this road. And—and that was why I walked along it. To—to meet you. Oh, dear heart," she sighed as I drew her very close to me, "from the very first, it was *I* who always sought *you!*—I who ever wished for you! Who ever heard of so one-sided a love affair?"

"And, to the last," I murmured happily, "it shall be *I* who shall follow wherever *your* dainty footsteps lead. They will lead me to such happiness as never mortal knew!"

THE END.

Appendix

This novel originally ran in four installments of Argosy magazine, from the December 1910 through the March 1911 issues.

December 1910: Chapters I through VII
January 1911: Chapters VIII through XI
February 1911: Chapters XII through XVI
March 1911: Chapters XVII through XVIII

Front text, Argosy, December 1910:
Author of "When Liberty Was Born," "The Spy of Valley Forge," "From Flag to Flag," etc.

A Story of Revolution Days Which Brings in the Figure of an Enemy for Whom All Cherish Only the Kindliest Feelings.

[The above front text was repeated on the opening pages of the 2nd, 3rd, and 4th installments of this serial.]

Front text, Argosy, January 1911:
SYNOPSIS OF CHAPTERS PREVIOUSLY PUBLISHED.
THE story is told by Captain Philip Wayne, attached to Benedict Arnold's staff near Cold Spring on the Hudson. Dissatisfied with slowness of promotion, he vents his ill temper on Edith Bliss, governess in the Arnold household, is reproved for his ill manners by a mysterious stranger who suddenly appears while they are picknicking on the Neutral Ground, and has his sword neatly whisked out of his grasp by this same individual. Later Mistress Bliss finds a paper behind the Arnold hat-rack which seems to breathe of conspiracy against the Cause. She passes it on to Wayne, who in turn shows it to Arnold. The latter bids him never speak of the thing, but the captain is on the lookout for clues to the identity of the traitor, and one night thinks he has one when he sees a cloaked figure steal out in a boat, to be followed a little later by a similar form in another skiff. Wayne takes a third boat in pursuit, but can keep track only of the second figure, which he follows across the Hudson to a point just below West Point. Among the bushes on shore, Wayne sees his prey meet a figure that is not cloaked, then the moon breaks from behind a cloud, a twig snaps under the captain's foot, the

cloaked figure turns toward him and he sees it is Edith Bliss. And the recognition of the man with her causes Wayne to spring toward him with a snarl.

Front text, Argosy, February 1911:
SYNOPSIS OF CHAPTERS PREVIOUSLY PUBLISHED.
The story is told by Captain Philip Wayne, attached to Benedict Arnold's staff near Cold Spring on the Hudson. Dissatisfied with slowness of promotion, he vents his ill temper on Edith Bliss, governess in the Arnold household, is reproved for his ill manners by a mysterious stranger who suddenly appears while they are picknicking on the Neutral Ground, and has his sword neatly whisked out of his grasp by this same individual. Later Mistress Bliss finds a paper behind the Arnold hat-rack which seems to breathe of conspiracy against the Cause. She passes it on to Wayne, who in turn shows it to Arnold. The latter bids him never speak of the thing, but the captain is on the lookout for clues to the identity of the traitor, and one night thinks he has one when he sees a cloaked figure steal out in a boat, to be followed a little later by a similar form in another skiff. Wayne takes a third boat in pursuit, but can keep track only of the second figure, which he follows across the Hudson to a point just below West Point. Among the bushes on shore, Wayne sees his prey meet a figure that is not cloaked, then the moon breaks from behind a cloud, a twig snaps under the captain's foot, the cloaked figure turns toward him and he sees it is Edith Bliss. And the recognition of the man with her causes Wayne to spring toward him with a snarl. But he quickly decides not to make a scene with the girl present, for he realizes that she loves this man, at the same time he admits to himself that he loves her. Then General Arnold appears and Edith departs, leaving Wayne to introduce the stranger, who supplies his name as John Anderson. Wayne then takes him for the spy, but Arnold explains that there are many John Andersons, and later bids Wayne guide the fellow on his way to New York, where he is going on a mission for the Cause. In spite of his jealousy, Wayne comes to like the fellow, and is sorry to part with him. Then on his homeward ride, he meets Edith, who bids him wildly bring Anderson back to her. Turning quickly about, he gallops southward again and finds Anderson captured by three Americans, who insist that he is a British spy. Wayne tries to

convince them to the contrary, but without avail, so starts back to get convincing proof from Arnold.

[There was no synopsis on the opening page of the final installment, Argosy, March 1911.]

Other books available
from the Silver Creek Press

2006

The Park Avenue Hunt Club:
The Silver Creek Edition
by Judson Phillips and Rodney Schroeter
(Available from the publisher)

(The following are available from the major bookstores online,
both as hardcopy books and as e-books.)

2015

The Flood Fighters, by Albert Payson Terhune
A novel first serialized in Country Gentleman magazine in 1920,
published under a pseudonym and not reprinted until the above edition.

An Albert Payson Terhune Reader
27 stories by Terhune from pulp magazines of the 1910s and 20s,
featuring all original illustrations.

Forthcoming

More work by Albert Payson Terhune
that has never been reprinted since its original publication.

More pulp fiction from the early 20th Century

www.ingramcontent.com/pod-product-compliance
Lightning Source LLC
Chambersburg PA
CBHW071010120726
47910CB00004B/1453